JAILBREAK

Pyro escapes from the penitentiary and into his former criminal associates' getaway car. The gang has been promised a share of the fortune Pyro hid away before being caught. But before heading for the buried cache, Pyro orders a detour to Onnaville, where he blackmails a plastic surgeon into giving him a new face. Ruthlessly, he then murders the surgeon, before running out on his gang. After all, how could they recognise him now? *But Nemesis was at hand . . .*

Books by John Robb
in the Linford Mystery Library:

ROBBERY WITHOUT VIOLENCE

JOHN ROBB

JAILBREAK

Complete and Unabridged

LINFORD
Leicester

First published in Great Britain

First Linford Edition
published 2011

British Library CIP Data

Robb, John.
    Jailbreak. - -
(Linford mystery library)
1. Criminals- -Fiction. 2. Fugitives from
justice- -Fiction. 3. Surgery, Plastic- -
Fiction. 4. Plastic surgeons- -Crimes
against- -Fiction. 5. Suspense fiction.
6. Large type books.
I. Title II. Series
823.9'2–dc22

ISBN 978–1–44480–573–4

Published by
F. A. Thorpe (Publishing)
Anstey, Leicestershire
Set by Words & Graphics Ltd.
Anstey, Leicestershire
Printed and bound in Great Britain by
T. J. International Ltd., Padstow, Cornwall

This book is printed on acid-free paper

1

The bell in the distant penitentiary clock struck eleven times. In five minutes Pyro was due to make his jailbreak.

He was digging an irrigation ditch — he, and around seven hundred other prisoners — it was supposed to be useful work.

The governor figured it gave the boys some kind of interest in life, to take them outside the penitentiary walls, and have them sweat among the cotton fields. You dug a couple of long, deep furrows down the slope. Then a couple more cross-wise. That way you conserved the rainfall which was nice for the planters, but it wasn't so nice for the guys who did the digging.

Pyro straightened his back and looked towards the highway. He gave out a low-pitched curse, that wasn't just nerves.

He always cursed when he toiled here, and saw the thin strip of road. Outside work didn't make a guy feel less of a prisoner. Hell, no! Seeing freedom so close made him feel that much worse! That was the trouble — you felt it a whole lot more than when you were shut up inside those walls. It was like a hungry guy who gets along okay until he smells a meal cooking.

Pyro figured he still had three more minutes to go.

Three minutes before the boys would come along the highway in a big roadster. Three minutes before the plan started to work — if it worked.

His throat was dry and there was a pounding of blood in his head, but that didn't matter. It was natural. It showed he was primed and ready for action. There'd be no mistake. Not if Lex and the rest of the outfit played their end of the deal right, and there was no reason why they should ball it up. They knew the pitch. It had been timed and checked to the last second. One of the guards, who had a short Thompson sub-machine gun slung over a shoulder, came up and gave Pyro a grin, but with no humour in it. 'Maybe

2

you find this work too much for yer constitootion. Maybe you figure yer entitled to a long rest.'

Pyro put a hand to his forehead. 'And maybe you're right,' he said. 'I ain't feelin' so good.'

The guard laughed. He was going to enjoy this. 'Gee! I sure am sorry about that. Would yer like me to fetch you a nice drink of somethin' hot?'

From afar off, Pyro heard the sound of an automobile. He resisted the temptation to glance along the highway. That might give the guard a hint. So far, things were working to schedule. Now a lot depended on the guys who were due to start a fight. He gripped his spade and thrust it deep into the soil.

'It looks like you've made a fast recovery, the guard sneered, 'but I guess big-time mobsters like you have just gotta be tough.'

He was going to say some more, but he changed his mind about that. A few prisoners further along the line had started beefing. One had accused another of delivering a kick on the ankle. Right now, the accuser was hopping around on one foot and making a whole lot of noise in the process. The others were taking sides. The guard groaned wearily. This' kind of thing often happened. They were like so many kids.

He bawled to them, 'Hey! Break it up!'

This time they didn't break it up. Suddenly one guy took a wild slug at another. Then the rough house got going.

Inside a few seconds twenty of them were beating hell out of each other — or so it seemed. Pyro decided that these boys were playing their parts well, but it was no trouble to them.

They were kind of pleased to help a guy who'd got a breakout organised.

The guard started to unsling his Thompson and with his other hand he groped for his whistle, so as to call aid from the other squatties who were stretched along the line. That was the moment Pyro was waiting for. He tossed up a spadeful of soil into the guard's face. His features disappeared under a cake of dirt. But Pyro didn't stop there. He twisted the implement round and brought it down in a wide arc on the guy's head. His peaked cap squashed down flat over the skull. He turned a half-circle before starting to fall.

Pyro was quite a stretch past the physical prime of life, and he hadn't been in the penitentiary long enough to lose all of his big pot-belly, but he could still move quickly. He caught the guard before he touched ground. Supporting him for a moment, he wrenched the gun from his arm, then turned towards the road. It was okay. The fight was still going on. The roadster was waiting right opposite him with the rear door open. The boys would be covering him in case any slugs started to fly in his direction.

That was the only real risk now — bullets from the guards.

Speed was what was needed. Speed in covering those three hundred yards to the car. He'd covered half of them. Still there was no shooting, although there was plenty of bawling going on behind him. Maybe the guards hadn't seen him yet. The boys back there would make it difficult for them to see much. They'd make plenty use of the excitement to crowd and jostle the guards.

There were always a few squatties placed well away from the working line. They wouldn't be jostled. Maybe they'd see him before he reached his objective.

There had been a heavy rainfall the previous day and the soil was soft. It pulled at the muscles so his legs pained with each rushing step, but he was nearly there. He could see their faces — Dal behind the wheel — Lex right beside him — Rick at the back —

Some earth spattered up almost direct in front of his face. They had seen him They were shooting now! Those slugs were falling close. Maybe this was where he oughta use the Thompson. Turn round and fire back so as to make them take cover. He was going to do just that when he heard Lex's voice. Lex was bawling: 'Keep goin'. You can make it!'

Lex was right. Only twenty yards now. More soil was thrown up but those bullets were several feet to his left. Their aim was getting worse as the range got longer.

The roadster's engine was revving to a

roar. It was easing forward. Two hands came out through the rear door. They grabbed his shoulders and threw him on to the carpeted floor. There was a jolt as Dal suddenly stepped on the gas pedal. He was up into second gear. Now into top and the tyres were screeching as they took a bend.

He'd made it. He was not going to serve a life term in a penitentiary. He was out after just three months. As he dragged himself onto the seat Pyro started to laugh.

2

Breaking out of a penitentiary only takes a guy halfway. Unless he knows where he's going after that, he'll find himself making a swift return trip. Then he'll spend quite a time sitting in the icebox, which is a private cell measuring two feet by three without a window or any light. In that place a guy can contemplate his folly and he has to stand upright while he's doing it.

Pyro didn't have that kind of ambition. His breakout took him all the way. It took him to a nice quiet house that stood distant from any place, at the edge of a lake, and with a deep forest behind it. The house was only twelve miles from the state penitentiary, which was smart. It meant they reached it in under fifteen minutes, so they didn't have to worry about switching cars, or avoiding highway patrols. They were clear out of circulation before the cops had got themselves organised. When the hunt really got going, it would be concentrated on areas a whole lot further off than this lonesome house. It had been a slick move to rent it!

None of them spoke much until Dal had guided the car up the long and weedy drive. When they were getting out Lex said, 'This car's gonna have a nice coat of paint — black paint this time, and the genuine licence plate is goin' back on it.' That part was Dal's assignment. They left him to deal with it in the garage while they went into the house.

The boys had rented the place through an agent, and paid all the dough in advance, so not many questions were asked.

It was nicely furnished with a lot of thick carpets and deep chairs scattered around on the ground floor, but at first Pyro wasn't in any condition to appreciate that sort of luxury. He took himself upstairs, had a shower, then changed out of his grey penal clothes into one of his own suits. It had been thoughtful of the boys to remember about bringing his own wardrobe along.

When he came down he was feeling a new guy. Like the old Pyro. The bub who rode the rackets. Who had got Onnaville City so nicely fixed that the cops almost saluted him in the streets. That was the way it had been — until those cripe-loused Feds had moved in and hammered him for that life sentence on a second-degree murder charge.

Lex and Rick were sucking bourbon around a miniature bar that was installed in a corner of the room. It was a well-stocked bar, but that didn't surprise Pyro any. His outfit always took good care of their comfort. Pyro took a drink from Lex and swallowed it fast. It tasted good — but kind of strange. Same with the cigarette that Rick gave him. It was funny, but when you were in the big house you spent a lot of time thinking about liquor and smokes. In a yearning sort of way you tried to imagine what it'd be like to have as much of the stuff as you wanted again. Then when you did have it, well it just didn't have as much kick as you'd expected. Maybe that was because you expected too much. Anyway, it still tasted okay.

'You can gimme another.' Pyro looked at Lex while the glass was being refilled. Lex was a bit tense and anxious. Like all the muscles of his high and strong frame were still bunched for action. That was natural. It'd been a big operation that they had just completed.

It was the same with Rick. Except that Rick was fidgetting. He kept licking his thin lips and stubbing out half-smoked cigarettes to light new ones. Rick didn't come as tough as Lex in some ways, but he was okay. He'd been a college boy, and he could talk good, which was sometimes useful.

Pyro knew, however, that it wasn't just the memory of the breakout that was making the boys raw, they had something else on their minds. It was the thought of two hundred grand in small bills and bearer bonds. That kind of dough would weigh heavy on any guy's mind, and it wasn't so long before they got around to talking about it.

Lex said, 'I figure we'll stay right here until the heat's cooled off. There's no need for any of us to move out for a couple of weeks. We've stocked up with plenty of supplies. After that, I guess we'll cut the dough four ways and scram.'

Pyro didn't answer. He just turned his fleshy face on Lex and grinned. Lex sucked in some more bourbon and asked, 'What's eatin' you? That's how we're gonna handle this, ain't it?'

Pyro cleared his throat. This was the moment when the boys were going to take it rough. They'd had the idea that they'd only gotta pull him out of the pen to get a share in the currency he'd got salted away. Right now, they were going to find out that something else was needed of them first. Something that would mean a whole lot of delay.

'There ain't gonna be any share-out yet a while,' Pyro said smoothly.

There were a few moments of heavy silence while the information was absorbed. Lex's mean eyes narrowed and he looked thoughtfully at the opposite wall. Rick ceased fidgeting and stared right at Pyro. In his college boy tones he said, 'I don't understand you, Pyro. We've got you out.

That's our part of the deal. Your end is to unearth that money you've got hidden some place and split it among us. There's no reason for any delay after the heat's off.'

Although he was feeling weary, Pyro stood up. He always talked better when he was standing. He faced a big oval mirror that was hanging over the fireset, and studied his reflection carefully.

'You can quit admiring your profile. If that pan of yours pleases you, then you're darned easy to satisfy. We wanta talk about our end of the dough,' Lex growled. In the old days he never would have dared speak in that way. Not when Pyro had his full mob around him, and just about ran Onnaville City. It seemed Lex was getting too confident. He'd have to be toned down a few shades. Not yet, though. There'd be plenty of time.

Pyro went on studying himself, then he said, 'I ain't admiring myself, Lex. I'm kinda worried.'

'Worried! You ain't got a thing to worry about.'

'I guess I have, Lex. It's this mug of

mine. It's sorta famous.'

Rick got his drink. 'I know how you're feeling, Pyro. After today your picture'll be slapped on to every newspaper in the States, but if you play smart you won't be recognised. You'll have enough money to settle some place a long way off, and you can always grow a beard.'

Pyro turned to face him. He was still grinning as he indicated the top of his bald skull and rubbed a hand round his smooth chin.

'That's one of my troubles. I don't grow enough hair to make a beard. Never did. And I ain't got any on top that can be dyed a new colour. It's gonna be mighty hard for me to change my appearance.'

Lex, who had been listening carefully, wasn't showing much sympathy. 'You'll have to take that chance,' he said. 'We ain't stickin' around this place for more'n a couple of weeks.'

Suddenly Pyro's voice was on ice. 'You're makin' a big mistake there, Lex. You're stayin' here until it's safe for me to leave. Maybe you're forgetting that I'm the guy who knows where the dough is?'

For a fraction of a second it looked as though Lex was going to act tough. He bunched his big fists and took a half-step forward, but there was something about Pyro that stopped him. Maybe it was flat hardness in his eyes, and the way his fatted mouth had become pressed into a shapeless slit. They were warnings that a few months in a penitentiary hadn't weakened Pyro any.

'Don't even think of doin' that again, Lex boy. There ain't no pay off in that kind of attitude. Now I wanta talk to you all the serious way. Get Dal outa the garage. I want him in here, too.'

Dal, who was in overalls, had, judging by their appearance, already started operations with the paint spray. He was a little crumb, was Dal. Not much higher than a good man's navel, but he didn't scare easy. He could handle a car, too.

When they'd fixed themselves with drinks and were sprawling in the deep chairs, Pyro started to talk. He paced around as he did so, using plenty of gesture like a Congressman at an election convention.

'You bums are sitting sweet,' Pyro told them. 'You ain't hunted men and no one knows you fixed the breakout for me, but with me it's a whole lot different. Every cop, and every smart guy in America's gonna be on the lookout for me, and I ain't gonna be so difficult to recognise. There's somethin' kinda distinctive about my pan. So what does that add up to? I'll tell you. Right now, fixed like I am, I wouldn't get away. I wouldn't have a chance. It might take weeks or months, but they'd pull me in some time.'

He paused to see how they were taking it, and figured 'cautiously' was the answer. Like an audience listening to a travelling salesman and waiting for the smart catch.

Pyro went on: 'That's where you boys are gonna help out. I'm gonna have my appearance changed.'

Lex grunted. Then he said: 'What the hell! That's just what Rick's been tellin' you, and you said you couldn't do it.'

Pyro nodded. 'Sure. But I'm not thinking about tryin' to disguise myself. I

16

ain't got anything so corny as that in my mind.'

'Okay, let's have it. What do you have in mind?'

'An operation.'

'You're crazy,' Lex told him. 'You'd be recognised just as soon as you walked into any hospital.'

'I don't aim to go to a hospital. The operation's gonna be done right here in this house.'

There was another period of silence. The three hoods looked dully at Pyro. It was broken when Rick said: 'That sounds fine. D'yuh know a right guy?'

Pyro shrugged his shoulders. He looked as though he was enjoying this. Any guy enjoys knowing all the answers 'I guess I do. He's called Doc Juruski. He was once a big number in plastic surgery. He'll do it okay — and he won't talk.'

Rick asked him why. Pyro was ready with that answer, too.

'Because he ain't supposed to be in the States, He's a Pole and he was eased in here illegally. It seems things weren't so comfortable for him in Poland and he

17

wanted to come here because he has relatives around. I know this, because I took a hand at getting' him in — in return for some sweet sugar. I figure Doc Juruski will do the job on my pan outa sheer gratitude. If he don't — then it'll be just too bad. If the cops get to know about him I guess he'll be shipped back home.'

They all understood the pitch now. None of them liked it.

Lex said, 'Listen, bud, we ain't actin' as nursemaids while you have your pan lifted. We've done our end of the deal, so I figure you oughta get that dough first and hand us our end. After that, you can have a new facial every day, and we won't worry any.'

Pyro took a few heavy steps to where Lex was sitting. He stopped within a few inches of his chair. He spoke direct to Lex but his words were intended for all of them.

'Get this,' he rasped. 'I need you guys here, and it's here that you're gonna stay if you wanta see a cut in that dough. If any of you wanta quit, you can blow right now and drop fifty grand. If you feel you can afford to lose that kinda dough, go ahead. If not, stick around, and do like I say.'

Lex was cringing a bit under this barrage. He was a lot bigger than Pyro and physically tougher.

'This wasn't in the deal,' he said. 'You promised to split the bucks if we got you out — '

Pyro interrupted. 'So I will — when my pan's changed so I won't be recognised. When that's done, I'll collect the dough and share it out like I said, but until then you boys ain't gonna get even a hint of where it is.'

They knew he wasn't kidding. Those boys were hungry for that dough, which was what Pyro had saved out of the racket proceeds. He'd managed to ice it out some place before his arrest by the Feds. With some guys you could get tough and slug the information out of them. Not with Pyro. He wasn't the sort to break under that kind of pressure.

It was Rick who voiced what they were all thinking. 'There doesn't seem much we can do about it,' he told Pyro. 'None of us like delay, so I guess we'd best make arrangements for this doctor to operate right away. The sooner your mug is changed, the sooner we'll have our padding.'

Pyro nodded approval. Rick might be a college boy, and he might look a piece sloppy with his pale movie star features but he had something above his ears besides solid bone

'You talk wise,' he said. 'And it's you, Rick, that's gonna contact Doc Juruski. This is how you're gonna do it.'

★   ★   ★

Doctor Juruski was alone in his surgery. The last patient had gone, and now he was pulling on his worn coat and humming a few bars of music he remembered from his student days. He felt tired, but tired in an agreeable way. Soon he'd be home and his housekeeper would be dishing up a supper. After that, if there were no calls on urgent cases, he'd spend the evening at the piano playing Polish music.

Music was quite a consolation to him. It took his mind off the fact that he was not supposed to be working here in the States either as a doctor or anything else. It made him temporarily forget that he, once a noted expert in plastic surgery, now had to toil as an ordinary practitioner. He had to do even that in a discreet kind of way in the poorer end of Onnaville. He hadn't to let his practice get too big, or else some folk might start wondering where he came from —

The bell buzz sounded on his surgery door.

The Doc swore mildly. 'Yes, come in,' he called.

There certainly did not seem to be much the matter with the guy who ambled towards him. Not physically, anyway, but he had the drawn appearance of a man who lives hard and wrong. As Rick took a gander at Doc Juruski he decided that Pyro had been right. This little medical man who blinked at him through thick, rimless spectacles would be easy to handle. He'd scare without a lot of cause. Rick decided to get right to the point. 'Pyro's sent me. He's got a job for you. It's a big job.'

The Doc's brow furrowed, as though he could not at first place the name. That was not surprising. It was years ago that the big-time hood had fixed his illegal entry into the country.

'Pyro? I do not — '

'You do. He was a help to you once.'

It came back to him. The Doc's expression changed from one of puzzlement to astonishment. 'I — recall Mister Pyro — but is he not in prison? I read in the newspaper — '

Rick grinned and pushed Doctor Juruski into a chair. 'He was in the big house, but he's out now.'

'So soon! He — he is to be congratulated.'

Rick agreed about that, but he didn't waste any more time. He gave out the whole pitch. He gave it in fast, crisp sentences, so he would not have to explain anything twice. When he had done, Juruski made a feeble gesture with one of his fine shaped hands.

'But what you ask — it is impossible.

Already I have broken the law to come into this country. If — if I do this I would be yet more — '

Rick knew how to handle this kind of objection. He'd been expecting it, and Rick could talk. 'If you don't do it, you'll be shipped right back to Poland, and I guess there'll be a hot reception committee waiting for you there. You're more than just an illegal immigrant, Doctor. You've been practicing medicine without a permit. It'd be tough for you if Uncle Sam was tipped off.'

Juruski gave out something that was like a whimpering groan. 'You can't expect this of me! I paid all I had to be brought into this country. Pyro can't do it!'

Rick wasn't moved a little bit. Since he'd first turned bad as a college student there had not been a lot of emotion in Rick. 'Pyro can and he will. He's expecting to see you this very night. If he doesn't he'll be sore, and you don't want him to feel that way about you, do you, Doc?'

The doctor made one more attempt.

'But I can't operate this way at such short notice. You say he's in a lonely house. That place will not be equipped. I haven't the instruments.'

'You've got money, haven't you? This is a chance to use some of it. I guess you'll be able to buy most of what you need in this town. Pyro ain't bothered about a lot of refinements. He just wants a change of appearance. He's turned modest since he broke out of the pen.'

There was a long pause. It ended when Juruski stretched out his hand to the telephone. He spun the dial and a woman's voice answered. He said: 'Listen, I've been called away on an urgent case. I won't be back for a week or two — no don't worry about my clothes. I haven't time to collect them. I'll buy all I need — I'll explain when I get back.'

He looked like a doomed man as he followed Rick out of the surgery.

3

Pyro was scared. The Doc had been at the house for a couple of days now. One of the bedrooms was being fitted out as an operating theatre. That had required more equipment than he'd expected. The Doc and Rick had been forced to make several trips into a distant town to make the purchases. They had not returned to Onnaville for this purpose in case Juruski was recognised by someone who knew he was supposed to be away. Quite a change had come over the Doc. He'd got over his first despair. Now it was almost as though he was looking forward to working on Pyro's pan. Somehow that seemed unnatural, and Pyro asked him about it.

Juruski held up his hands. Those long, fine hands. 'I spent a lifetime training these for surgery,' he said. 'But for years I've not been able to use that skill. Do you wonder that, in spite of everything, I welcome this opportunity.'

Pyro was slightly reassured. Then he asked, 'You can fix me so no one'll know me?'

Juruski nodded emphatically. 'It will be easy. Your features are fat. There is much material on which to work. I will operate tomorrow.'

'That's fine,' Pyro said uncertainly. 'But when'll I be able to step out?'

'You will be in bandages for — perhaps three weeks. Perhaps a month. There must be time for the incisions to heal.'

Pyro felt a dryness in his throat. Like he'd felt just before he'd broken from the penitentiary guard. At one time the idea of this operation had seemed easy enough to him. He knew that a whole lot of folks had it done when they had been in bad accidents, and Juruski was a top guy at the job — or he had been. At first, there had not seemed to be a thing to worry about, but now the time was close, he saw it in different way.

Supposing the Doc balled it up? Or supposing he didn't recover? Pyro felt an ooze of sweat seeping down his forehead. This prospect was something new to him.

Something he didn't like. He'd be stretched on that operating table he'd seen taken up. He'd be unconscious. He wouldn't know a thing of what was going on. Juruski would be working on him — working on him with knives and hell knows what else. This wasn't like ordinary danger. Not like facing out with a guy with a gun.

Like all of his kind, Pyro was yellow deep down. He looked as if he had plenty of what it takes when the game was playing his way, and when plenty of roughneck brutality would swing the balance, but strong-arm stuff wouldn't help him any once he was under the anaesthetic. Pyro knew it, and the yellow was emerging from the slimy depths.

He decided to take out a kind of insurance policy on himself. A policy based on fear. He said to Juruski: 'It'd be too bad for you if I don't come outa this okay.'

Lex and Rick had eased into the room. Pyro was glad of that. He wanted the boys to know what he had in mind. Juruski's tones were quavering when he asked:

'What do you mean? There isn't a lot of danger in this sort of operation and you're in good condition. You'll be all right.'

'I sure am glad to hear it,' Pyro told him. 'Y'see, my outfit have a hunch it's mighty important for me to come through okay. If I don't, they'll be facing a future without much dough, and I guess that'd make them real mad with you — get me?'

Doc Juruski got him. He said in a low voice: 'You'll be fine. I don't kill many patients.'

Somehow that didn't give Pyro a lot of comfort.

★ ★ ★

Pyro didn't need to worry. For the first couple of days after the Doc had worked him over he had not felt so good. He figured he'd never get used to having his pan swathed in bandages so everything was covered except his eyeballs and a slit for his mouth, but that was a minor inconvenience when compared with the fact that the job was done. When those bandages were removed he'd have a new appearance. He'd be able to go any place without being recognised. He'd have to fix himself another identity, but that would be easy.

As he lay in bed he got through a lot of steady thinking. He put his thoughts into words when the Doc was checking him over on a morning a week after the operation. 'I guess a guy like you can't have much dough. The way you're fixed, there ain't much opportunity for pullin' in the bucks.'

Doc Juruski nodded. 'You're right. But I make enough to get along and no more. Paying for all the equipment needed here has cost me a lot, though. I know you won't pay me for this job, but I'm hoping you'll settle my expenses.'

'Maybe I can do better than that,' Pyro said, his voice muffled under the heavy swathings. 'Maybe you could use fifty grand.'

Juruski blinked as though at first he did not understand. 'Fifty thousand dollars! That's a fortune!'

'Sure it's a fortune. It can be yours if

you act wise. Are you interested?'

'The man who's not interested in fifty thousand bucks has not been born,' Juruski answered.

'You talk smart,' Pyro said. 'Maybe you've figured that I've got a lot of sugar tucked away, and my outfit's waiting for a cut in it when I'm ready to move.'

'Yes. That's obvious.'

'But when them three bums have had their slice of the cake there won't be so much left for me — '

Juruski got the drift. He was near to being horrified. He was a simple soul. 'But they got you out of the penitentiary! Surely you promised them a share for doing that?'

There was no trace of sympathy in Pyro's muffled tone. 'Sure I promised them that. But what of it? They're a bunch of no-goods. They'll just sling the dough around if they get their claws on it, and they'll be flat again inside of a few months, but if you got a nice slice you wouldn't waste it, would you, Doc?'

Juruski was thinking fast. He was thinking of his furtive existence since coming to the States. Until he'd been able to set up a discreet medical practice, he'd been supported by his niece, Rhona. She lived a little way out of Onnaville and, except for the Pyro outfit, was the only person who knew he had no permit to be in the States. Rhona was a good kid. She was the only child of a brother who had emigrated to America a long time ago and died a few years back.

He remembered that Rhona was going to be wed sometime soon. To a newspaper guy. Neither of them had a lot of money. But fifty thousand! With that he'd be able to help them and repay what she'd done for him. Doc Juruski was no natural crook. Normally he was as honest as they come, but right now he was faced with one hard fact. It was that he'd already broken the law, maybe unwillingly, but the law doesn't take much account of motives.

Through the slits in his bandages Pyro watched the tense set of the Doc's face. He had a hunch of what was going on in that mind, and decided to throw out some more bait.

'With fifty thousand maybe you could fix yourself with a proper permit to work in the States. You could hire smart lawyers. Top grade guys. They can do a lot — if they're paid the right currency.'

Juruski was one hundred per cent human and no form of humanity could ignore this offer. 'What do we do?' he asked.

★   ★   ★

Pyro cut the delay. With a guy of uncertain nerves like the Doc for an ally, it was best to move fast. That was why he aimed to get clear of the house on the following day.

Dal did all the cooking for the household of five. If it could be called cooking. The kitchen was so full of canned foods that it looked like a general store. All the meals came out of those cans. Dal's culinary operations consisted of heating the contents.

At breakfast he served up canned ham, canned tomatoes, canned beans. The tomatoes and the beans looked like they'd suffered from some disease that had called for a lot of blood letting. Lex and Rick looked at the stuff without enthusiasm. They pushed the plates away untasted and bawled for the coffee.

It was a habit of Dal's to leave the coffee until last. The boys always had to remind him they were waiting. They reminded him now, but this time Doc Juruski saved him the trouble of the trip. 'I'll get it,' he said, rising from the table. 'I guess Dal doesn't get much rest.'

This was old world courtesy. It was something new to the boys. As Juruski went out Dal said, 'That old quack must be nuts.'

The coffee percolator was standing on the table, filled and ready for drinking. The Doc removed the glass top. His hand was shaking a bit as he took a small phial from his jacket pocket, uncorked it, then carefully poured three drops of the blue liquid into the coffee. He stirred this refreshment with a spoon before taking it into the room. As he put it before the boys he said, 'Pyro's calling for me. I must go. Don't drink it all.'

Lex poured himself the first cup, stiffening it with plenty of brown sugar. Rick followed. They both drank fast. Dal was about to raise his own cup to his lips when Lex grimaced. 'I'm old-fashioned,' he said. 'I like my coffee hot. This stuff's gotta crust of ice on it. Go heat it again.'

Dal felt at his cup. 'That quack musta taken the lid off,' he grunted. Without tasting his own, he picked up the percolator and took it back to the kitchen. Re-heating was not a big operation. He was back inside of three minutes. When he pushed into the room he saw something that made him stop dead.

Rick was lying on the carpet at the side of his chair, liked he'd just slowly rolled there. One arm was twisted under him and he was motionless.

Lex was still in his chair, but he'd slumped face forwards so he was partly supported by the table. He was out too. Like Rick, he looked as if he was going to stay that way for a long time.

Dal was only a little runt. There was nothing impressive about him. It's hard to be impressive when you're only sixty-two inches in your reinforced shoes, but there was nothing dumb about him. He didn't panic and start rushing upstairs to tell Pyro. Instead, he examined Rick and Lex carefully. He pulled up the lids of their eyes and saw the pupils, That told him what had happened. In the ordinary way, when eyelids are shut the pupils become big, but in their case they were as small as pinheads. That meant just one thing. It meant dope. He'd a hunch on where it had come from.

Dal groped under his jacket for his shoulder holster When he moved towards the stairs there was a gun in his right hand.

★ ★ ★

'How long before them drops start workin'?' Pyro demanded. He was dressed and sitting on the edge of the bed, but he didn't look so good. Not with those bandages still covering his pan.

'They'll have worked by now,' Juruski told him. 'I've used a strong drug, but tasteless. They'll be under about a minute after taking the first cup.'

Juruski had surprised Pyro. The Doc had shown far less sign of nerves than he'd expected. He thought it was amazing what the prospect of a thick slice of dough would do. It was even able to make this timid old guy tough. So tough that Pyro handed him a gun. 'You'd better have this. Right now, I can't see so well if there's any shootin'.'

The Doc didn't take it. He wasn't that tough. He blinked at the Luger like he'd never seen such a thing before. 'I don't want that. I — I didn't think there was any chance of shooting.'

'There ain't — if the dope's okay.'

'The dope can't fail — but I'm not taking part in violence. In any case, I don't know how to use one of those things.'

Pyro dropped the gun back in his pocket. 'Okay,' he said. 'Have it your way. I'm kinda relying on you right now. Let's get outa this dump.'

Because Pyro could not see much, Doc Juruski led the way. There should have been no need for silence. They believed there was no need for it, but, instinctively, they moved quietly down the passage to the stairhead. Neither spoke during that part of the journey.

When they reached the top of the staircase, Doc Juruski looked down: first at their goal, which was the door at the opposite end of the hall. That door was open, and through it he could see the red gravel drive and a strip of the lawn beyond. The morning sun was shining out there. It looked kind of peaceful and inviting. Then he saw something else — a small guy putting his foot on the bottom step. A guy with a gun in his hand.

It was in that moment that Doc Juruski knew the hell of abject fear. His jaw unhinged. His throat swelled so he could give no warning to Pyro. He froze at the top of the stairs, a sweating palm gripping the balustrade. From directly behind him he heard Pyro say, 'What's holdin' you, Doc? We ain't got all — ' Dal's voice interrupted him. It came to them like the wrenching of a hasp. 'Were you guys goin' any place?'

Pyro eased sideways so that the Doc

did not interfere with his view. As he focussed his eyes through the slits in the bandages he let out a couple of comprehensive oaths. Then he said: 'Nope, we ain't goin' any place, Dal. The Doc said I'd be okay if I took a walk around. That's all.'

It sounded as convincing as a drink reform lecture in a downtown saloon, and Pyro knew it.

Dal continued to mount the stairs. He did so slowly, like he was enjoying the situation, and that gun of his was held very steady. 'Just a walk around, uh?' Dal said. 'It sure is a pity that Lex and Rick can't join you.'

It wasn't so smart of Dal to say that. Pyro was quick to absorb the fact that the dope had worked on the two others. He knew now that for some reason it was only this runt who had escaped its effects, and he realised something else. It was that Dal would never use that gun on him. Not while he alone knew the locality of the two hundred grand. Maybe the setup wasn't so bad. Pyro had a hunch he'd be able to handle Dal. In every way Dal was small-time.

'You're gettin' things wrong,' Pyro said. 'There ain't nothing to get sore about.'

He was getting used to peering through those slits. He was watching Dal carefully as he came up to them. Distances had to be nicely calculated.

Dal was saying: 'You ain't movin' outa this house. Not until we all go together. We've got an interest in you, Pyro. We don't wanta lose your company.'

Pyro shifted his stance slightly. Very slightly. Not enough for Dal to notice, but he arranged himself so his left hand was hanging behind the small of the Doc's back. Dal was only three steps from them now. It was here that he stopped.

He gestured with his gun. 'Get right back in your room — both of you bums. And you'd best stay there. I'm gonna be down here keeping watch until Lex and Rick wake up.'

Pyro gave a belly laugh. It sounded even deeper than usual because of the covering over his mouth. 'Sure we'll go back to my room if that's what you want, Dal. But the way I see it, you'd — ' He did not finish that sentence.

He'd never had any intention of finishing it. He broke off his flow of words as he slapped his left fist into Doc Juruski's back.

Some things can happen so fast that the eyes can't register the details. It was that way at this moment. The Doc gave a grunt that developed into a shriek as he was projected forward and slightly sideways in the direction of Dal.

Maybe the Doc shrieked because he knew that his life was in the balance. Dal had only to squeeze the trigger and the Doc would have no more interest in earthly problems, but Dal did not shoot — not until it was too late to do him any good, and the Doc any harm. Juruski crashed into his chest, knocking him backwards. Dal's arms went out instinctively to save himself. It was then that he pulled the trigger and damaged the wall about eight feet up. Then the two swayed for a second like boozed trapeze artists and went rolling down the long flight of stairs.

Pyro hadn't been wasting time. He had

his own gun out. Because his vision wasn't so good, he should have been careful about the way he followed them, but he was in no mood for caution. He made the descent three steps at a time. In spite of his weakened state, Pyro could still move. When he got to the bottom there was no need for him to do much. Only to help the Doc to his feet. Dal had hit his head against the wall while falling. He was out as cold as Lex and Rick. Doc Juruski was unhurt — in a physical sense, but his nerves weren't in such good shape: his entire body was shaking like he was having a fit, but Pyro didn't take a lot of notice of that. He grabbed the Doc's arm, and urged him through the front door.

The garage was at the side of the house. In it, the roadster waited. Dal had done a nice job in re-spraying the coachwork. It glistened like black ebony. Pyro pushed Juruski into the driving seat.

'Get movin',' he rasped.

The Doc didn't seem to hear him. He just sat there, rimless spectacles awry, face muscles pulsating. Pyro cursed.

'You've gotta drive this car. I can't. What's eatin' you? Are you scared? Well, there ain't anything to be scared about. Not now.'

The Doc groaned, but extended a trembling hand and switched on the ignition. His driving wasn't so good as they went down the long path towards the road. Twice he nearly piled them up against the spruce trees at either side, but they reached the highway okay. There the Doc's condition improved. 'Which way?' he asked Pyro.

'To Onnaville.'

That surprised the Doc but he still wasn't capable of asking too many questions. They were on a secondary highway, which, ten miles along, joined the main drag. By now Doc Juruski was feeling a lot better. He was keeping the roadster on a straight course. 'Where is this place we're going to?' he asked.

Pyro thought for a moment. Then he said, 'Stop the car. I wanta talk serious to you.' The car rolled to a halt at the roadside. Where does this dame of yours live?'

Juruski looked at the bandaged head in amazement. 'Dame of mine! What are you talking about? I don't have any — er — dame.'

Pyro produced his belly laugh. 'Sure you don't. I'm talkin' about that doll who's related to you somehow.'

'You — you mean my niece, Rhona?'

'Sure, that's who I mean. Rhona's a nice name. She lives some place just outa Onnaville, don't she?'

'She does,' Doc Juruski told him reluctantly. 'But what's that to do with you?'

'It's got plenty to do with both of us. That's where we're gonna stay until the time's right for you to take these damed bandages off my pan.'

The Doc gripped the steering wheel until the bones showed white in his thin hands. He turned and looked almost frantically at Pyro. 'Stay there! We can't stay with Rhona! That's impossible. What's your idea? I thought you'd got some place ready fixed. That's what you told me.'

Pyro's answer came fast. 'Sure I told

you that, and I wasn't telling no lies. I just forgot to tell you I aimed to stay at this particular hideout. The dame's got an apartment, ain't she?'

The Doc was too raw to do anything but nod. 'Sure she has. But she'll want to know why I've brought you there — maybe if I fixed you up to stay at my surgery — '

'That's no dice. Inside of a few hours the boys are gonna start lookin' for us. I have a hunch they're gonna be mighty sore about missin' the dough. Your surgery'll be one of the first spots they'll check.'

That information didn't reassure the Doc any. 'But if they traced us to Rhona's apartment — what then?'

'They won't trace us there. They don't even know you've gotta niece — now relax and look happy. This is the best way. It's the snuggest hideout of the lot. Your niece don't have to know a thing. You can even tell her some of the truth if it'll make you feel pure. Say you've changed my face because I'm a rich guy who finds it kinda monotonous when he sees himself in the mirror. You've done it the secret way because you daren't do it in the open, and you want me to stay there with you until this bandage muck can come off. That sounds mighty convincing to me.'

Doc Juruski pulled off his spectacles and started to polish them on a piece of rag from the dash box. He gathered himself for a last protest. It was like firing off a blank shell at half cock. 'I can't do this! I just can't! Rhona's a nice kid — she's gonna be married soon, too. I daren't risk it — ' His last words petered away like they were on a broken gramophone.

Pyro knew the answer. 'If you feel that way you won't see fifty grand,' he said. 'And it'd be too bad if the cops gotta know about you. D'you wanta be sent back to Poland, Doc?'

Doc Juruski was getting near to sobbing, but he started the roadster again and headed it on towards Onnaville.

4

Dave Arran yawned and wished he was some place else. He figured that right now he'd like to be with Rhona. Ot if that wasn't possible, he'd have no sort of objection to getting slowly drunk in some saloon. Anything was better than sloping around a newspaper office and not having any assignment to work on. He yawned again and tried to find some consolation in the thought that life was often like this. Too often.

Most folks seemed to have the crazy notion that a reporter's life consisted of nonstop action. Just beating around after stories that were hot — usually with a dame in tow. Folks got the notion from Hollywood. No one knew where Hollywood had got it from, Certainly not from a study of newspaper offices.

It was a hard fact, Dave thought, that most of a newspaper man's existence was made up of going after stories that would never see print because they'd never interest anybody. Or, as now, just sitting around and doing nothing because there was nothing to do. It wasn't an encouraging line of thought, but the truth doesn't often offer much encouragement.

The phone rang on his desk. That sound alone was a welcome break. The next sound was still more welcome. It was Rhona at the other end of the line. She was wearing a hundred-buck diamond ring on her left hand. The ring he'd bought. He was due to meet her later, when he'd finished this round of merciless toil, but her voice was welcome at all times. That was the way he felt about her.

He wasn't so pleased when she said, 'Listen, honey, I can't keep that date tonight. It's my uncle. I can't give you the details right now, but if you'll come round to my apartment for some supper I'll explain.'

That seemed like a good consolation prize, even if Doc Juruski was going to be around. After he replaced the receiver Dave gave himself a cigarette. Having nothing else to do, he fell to thinking

47

about the Doc. Dave knew about his illegal entry into the States. Rhona had told him, with the Doc's permission, soon after he'd put that ring on her finger. She felt he ought to know, and Juruski had felt the same way.

The information was safe with Dave. Most reporters carry in their heads as many confidential facts as the President. Anyway he liked the Doc. Right now the States was mighty full of guys who had no legal standing there. Not all of them doing useful work like Juruski from Poland was doing.

The last half-hour before leaving the office was always the worst, particularly after a day like this. You spent eight hours hoping that something would happen. Then the last thirty minutes hoping it wouldn't, so you could get clear of the place on time.

Thirty minutes ticked by, Dave's opposite number arrived on the dot, and Dave drove to Rhona's apartment in his coupé. Her place was in a new suburb a few miles out of the centre of Onnaville. It was on the eleventh floor of a big block

48

of apartment buildings. She met him in the hall. It was there that she told him about the Doc bringing in a special kind of patient.

Dave said, 'Heck — the Doc sure is running some risk when he starts carrying out operations. And say — this apartment of yours ain't all that big to put up a couple of guys.'

Rhona shook her blonde head. 'It's big enough. They're sharing the spare room, but they'll have to look after themselves while I'm at the office.' She worked as a stenographer for an attorney. While the four of them were taking supper Dave's instinct, which newsmen and stray dogs live by, got to work. With reporters they call it a nose for news.

Dave noticed that the Doc had the jitters. He had them bad. The fact was obvious, even though he was trying out a lot of self control. Maybe that in itself did not surprise Dave much. In a way, it was natural. When an illegal immigrant carries out a secret operation, he can't be expected to relax immediately afterwards.

No, it was not just the Doc's jitters that

interested Dave. It was more than that. It was the fact that he seemed scared of his patient. Scared of this guy with bandages over his head who'd been introduced by some name like 'Mr. Teele'. Not that the patient said much. All that covering over one's pan was not conducive to flowing conversation, but Doc Juruski kept glancing at him in the way a rabbit might glance at a stoat.

Dave got through a lot of hard thinking and hard watching during that meal. Before he left, he said to Rhona: 'The Doc's on mighty thin ice. I've a hunch we don't know it all.'

'It's funny you saying that.' Rhona told him. 'I feel the same way and I'm worried.'

5

They were alone in the apartment. Pyro and the Doc. It had been that way for the couple of hours since Rhona had gone to her office. Juruski had finished a long examination in which he'd probed beneath those bandages. 'These things can come off. Your skin's healed fine. Quicker than I thought.'

Pyro had been in a deep chair. He stood up suddenly at that piece of information. 'You mean — my pan's okay?'

'That's what I mean,' Juruski told him. 'I'm going to take the bandages off now — just hold still — maybe this'll hurt a bit, but not much.' It hurt a lot. Several times Pyro winced and grunted. Juruski had been guilty of the optimism of all doctors, but Pyro didn't mind so much. It was in a good cause.

When it was over it seemed good to feel the air around one's pan again. Cautiously, he raised a hand to his skin. It felt strange. Like touching the face of some other person. The Doc was watching him with professional interest.

Pyro asked quietly, 'What do I look like?'

Doc Juruski gave a thin smile. 'Why not tale a peek in the mirror? I think I've done a good job on you.'

Pyro didn't go straight to the mirror. He was scared of taking a look at himself now the time had come. Wild fevered thoughts crowded his mind. Suppose the Doc had been two-timing? Suppose he'd made him look like some kinda monster? It'd be easy for the Doc to have done that. Easy to fix him so he was only fit for a freak show in a carnival! Maybe the Doc *had* done that! There was something darned unusual about the way he was grinning right now.

'If my pan isn't okay, I'll — '

Juruski cut in. His tones were almost sympathetic. 'I know how you're feeling. They all feel that way. Better look in the mirror and get it over!'

Pyro braced himself. His eyes were closed as he walked towards that glass.

They were still closed when he stopped a yard from it. He opened them very slowly. His eyelids felt heavy and tight. He was looking at a stranger. 'Hell — this ain't me. This is some other guy.'

That was how it seemed. He was looking at a face that was thin. Thin with high cheekbones. Everything had changed shape. His lips were smaller, maybe better. His nose had become straight and refined. Even his eyes were oval instead of — as they had been, round.

He gradually got over the first shock, and as he did so he realised an important fact. The new Pyro was not such a bad looking guy. He was an improvement on the old one. Pyro himself appreciated that fact. He had never kidded himself any about his looks. He turned to Juruski. 'You've done a good job, Doc. I don't recognise myself, so I guess nobody else will.'

The Doc forgot his fears. He beamed pleasure now. This was a matter of professional pride. 'I still have my skill,' he said simply. 'I wish I could use it more often. Perhaps with the money you're paying me I'll be able to fix American cirizenship.'

Pyro pulled the only cigarette he possessed out of his pocket. This was his first taste of tobacco since the operation. He was dragging hard as he said: 'Yeah — your dough. Didn't I say somethin' about fifty grand?'

Juruski nodded eagerly. 'Yes, that's the figure you fixed. I'll be able to do a lot with that money. Not only for myself, but Rhona as well. I'll be able to make up for what she's done for me.'

Pyro smiled. He said slowly, 'Yeah — maybe you would've been able to do that.'

'Would have? But I intend to. It'll be easy with that money.'

'It won't. You ain't gonna get that fifty grand. You ain't gonna get even fifty cents.'

The Doc ceased to beam. 'You can't do that. We made an agreement.'

'Sure we did. But it ain't an agreement now because I'm not seein' things the same way. You ain't gettin' any of my dough, Doc.'

Juruski was holding some of the

bandaging. He started to twist it in his hands like a hysterical girl with a handkerchief.

'You mean — I've done all this for nothing?'

Pyro dropped his half-finished cigarette on the carpet, ground it out with his heel, and cursed when he realised he had no more. There was a silver case on the table, however — he snatched it.

In a flat way Juruski said, 'That's Dave's cigarette case. He left it here the other night.'

Pyro tossed it back after he'd extracted a smoke. 'You're in a helluva spot, Doc. Maybe a worse kinda spot than ya know!'

The Doc wasn't listening. He was staring blankly out the window. Pyro's next words commanded his attention though!

'I'm gonna kill you.' The four words were uttered Pyro's most casual manner, but each had the ring of a funeral bell.

It was quite a while before the Doc could frame an answer. Then he said, 'You — you must be having a joke, Mister Pyro.'

'Nope, it ain't no joke. I'm gonna kill you.'

Juruski started to back towards the door that gave on to the living room.

'It ain't no good thinking; of gettin' out,' Pyro said. 'I've locked the hall door. The key's in my pocket. Maybe I'm a bit sorry about this, but I ain't havin' anyone around who knows what I look like. Not even you, Doc. I can't take that chance.'

Doc Juruski stopped retreating. He wiped sweat off his face with the bandages. 'If you shoot me it will be heard,' he said quietly.

'I ain't gonna shoot you. I'm gonna do it the quiet way. With my hands.'

Juruski said very slowly, 'You're going to need me, Pyro. The bandages are off and you look all right, but after these operations there is often a weakness in the eye muscles. It may not develop for a week or two, but when it does you'll need treatment.'

'Y'mean my lamps ain't gonna be okay?'

'They'll be okay, Mister Pyro, but they'll need this attention. You'll want me for that. You can't kill me.'

Pyro wasn't impressed. 'You ain't the only doc in the States,' he said. 'You could be kiddin', but even if you're not, I ain't worried. I can get some other quack to fix it.'

Juruski started backing again. Pyro, who was moving forward, was now within reach of him. His hands were coming up to grip the Doc's throat. Juruski's instinct of self-preservation ordered his lips and lungs to shout for help. He opened his mouth, but no sound emerged. Pyro pressed one strong hand round his windpipe. That was all he used. Just one hand. At first, it only exerted pressure. Soon it was also holding Juruski upright. It was when the Doc's face was purple and the tongue hanging out that Pyro knew the job was done. He relaxed his grip and the late Doc Juruski thudded to the floor.

★ ★ ★

Dave Arran had been out on a story, if that kind of assignment could be termed

57

a story. He'd been to interview an elderly woman who claimed to have exploded a hydrogen bomb in her backyard. She'd left for the bughouse before Dave had arrived. His return trip took him near to Rhona's apartment. And remembering the cigarette case he'd left there, he decided to collect it. He also figured he'd like the chance of again meeting the Doc and his patient. Without knowing why, he was not liking this setup.

Dave braked his coupé outside the apartment block and eased towards the main entrance. He went up in the self-operated elevator. The door of Rhona's apartment was direct opposite the elevator gates. He was stepping on to the corridor when the apartment door opened, and out came a guy with a fat body and an ill-fitting — because thin — face! He guessed it was someone who'd been calling on the Doc or the patient. He wondered who. No one was supposed know about those two visitors.

The fat guy brushed past Dave and got into the elevator fast. Too fast. Dave, wondering why he was in such a helluva hurry, watched him until he descended out of the range of his vision, then he pushed the buzz on the apartment door. Nothing happened. He pushed again. Not a sound of activity from inside. He turned the door handle, and stepped into the hall. He crossed to the lounge, and then he almost stepped on Doc Juruski.

He felt his belly heaving, like he was going to be sick. His brain was whirring. The wheels were going round, but nothing useful was happening. Then his mental equipment got back into gear. He went to the telephone, gave a brief — very brief on account of there being nothing more yet — report to the newsroom desks. Then he called the cops.

6

The inside staff of the *Onnaville Star* were never discouraged by lack of information. Give those boys a crumb and they'd bake a cake. A photographer arrived at the apartment only a few seconds after the first patrol car. He got a close-up picture of the body. Meantime, the paper's library had been doing some fast research into the background of the Joe. They needed to do this because Dave hadn't given them any of the Doc's personal details. The library soon discovered that they hadn't a reference at all on Doc Juruski. That puzzled them. Their files generally had some dope on guys of his class. So what! So they turned up the American Medical Directory. Every doctor legally in practice in the States was listed there. Anyway, every doctor who had a right ro practice — so I don't have to tell you what they didn't find! Then the copywriters got busy, and the headline man too!

It was all pushed through at a speed that would kill the kind of business tycoons who like to think of themselves as hustlers. The new edition was on the streets within seventy minutes of the Doc dying, and it was as top-grade sensation. Maybe it was a bit misleading, but the *Onnaville Star* was not the sort of paper to spoil a good story just for the sake of few minor details like facts.

The streamer head announced, *Mystery Doctor is Strangled in Girl's Apartment.*

That did no justice to Rhona.

The secondary headline asked, *Who Was The Quack Juruski?*

Dave was still at the apartment when he saw this edition. He'd spent most of the past hour answering questions from the cops, and not answering them too fully. The sight of his own newspaper decided him to give it all. It would all come out, anyway. He figured it'd be best if neither he nor Rhona tried concealing facts. Rhona agreed to that.

He'd half expected Rhona to fold under the shock, but she did not. She was bewildered and shaken, but that kid didn't fold easy. He left her to explain it all to the law while he got into a corner so as to phone his newspaper. The result was an improvement so far as the press was concerned. The next edition substituted the word *Niece's* for *Girl's* in the streamer head. It looked a whole lot more respectable, and it had the advantage of being true.

The secondary headline was switched completely. It now read: *Juruski Was Illegal Immigrant And Plastic Surgeon. Did Patient Slay Him?*

For the first two hours the apartment was as crowded as a close scrum in a ball game. Nearly all of the guys there were cops. Cops taking pictures, cops taking measurements, cops asking questions. The most prolific guy on the question angle was Captain O'Teefe. O'Teefe was in charge of the Homicide Bureau. He was a small guy with a face like a bird of prey, but there was nothing dumb about him. When most of the spot investigations were complete he eased up to Dave and Rhona. 'I figure you two had better come with me to headquarters.'

Rhona looked scared, but Dave reassured her. He told her maybe they just wanted a statement, and that was what Captain O'Teefe did want. He took one from each of them and they were counter-signed by witnesses. When that was done O'Teefe sat behind his desk and read them through. While doing this he had something of the appearance of an ill-tempered parrot looking at a dish of unwanted seed.

Then he looked up and regarded them with bleak eyes. 'I could hold both of you pending a thousand dollars bail,' he said. 'That's what I could do. Maybe you're wondering why. Okay, I'll tell you. The lady's been harbouring an illegal immigrant. That's against the law. You, mister newshawk, you've been aware of the presence of such an immigrant without declaring the fact. That's against the law, too, but I ain't gonna charge you. Not this time. It wouldn't be worthwhile.'

He tried to look magnanimous about it, but he didn't kid Dave, who knew why no charge was being brought. It was because if Dave or Rhona were held, Captain

O'Teefe would be in bad with the *Onnaville Star*, and in the long run a news-sheet can always break a cop. O'Teefe did not want to be broken.

Dave decided to ooze gratitude. Right now, it was the diplomatic line to take. He thanked O'Teefe. That pleased the police chief. He even grinned — but only for a moment. He was serious again as he said: 'I figure it's a buck to a peanut the killer is the guy who was in the bandages. The guy you saw coming out of the apartment. Remember, the Doc had taken those bandages off just before he died. We found some of the material still in his hands.'

That seemed like a good reason to Dave and he said so. There was no doubt that this cop was no cluck, but O'Teele's next words hit Dave like a series of short jabs from a heavyweight. He said, 'If I'm right, that could put you in a bad spot. It could mean you're the only living man who knows what the killer looks like. Whoever slew Juruski may suddenly realise he has a heck of an interest in keeping you quiet.'

★ ★ ★

The boys had been to work. From the time they'd first collected their fuddled wits they had toiled hard to pick up some trace of Pyro and the Doc. There had been a fiendish desperation about their efforts. Each of them had in mind that a whole lot of bucks were in the balance. The thought of that dough gave them plenty of inspiration. They cased the Doc's surgery. They cased the sleazy downtown joints. They even cased the hotels in and around Onnaville, because they had a hunch they wouldn't go far while Pyro was still in his wrappings.

All this didn't bring any kind of reward. Not until the time when they were about to throw up. The time when they had gathered, weary and cursing, in the quiet house and were drinking fast bourbons. Dal and Rick were slumped in deep chairs. They were thinking uncharitable thoughts. Dal was also rubbing his head at the spot where it had crashed against the wall. Lex, who was standing by the window looking like he didn't appreciate the view, suddenly said, 'To hell with this, we've been two-timed and there ain't a thing we can do about it.'

By way of something to do, he turned to the radio and switched it on. A guy with a syrupy voice was bleating about the virtues of a breakfast cereal. He finished by saying that the day's news flashes were being presented by courtesy of the folks who made the cereal. The boys were only half listening, but they gave the whole of their attention when the newscaster started to read out about the killing of Doc Juruski.

It was late afternoon and by now most of the facts were available. The mob listened in a dazed way. Particularly to the bit about the cops looking for the guy that Dave Arran had seen emerging from the apartment. Lex turned off the radio. 'We're gonna have a nice friendly talk with this Mister Arran,' he said. 'I figure he saw Pyro's new face. He can help us some.'

★ ★ ★

Pyro cursed himself. He did it efficiently, sparing nothing. He was sitting in a corner of a quiet saloon. He had turned into this joint almost immediately after leaving the apartment. It had been a change of plan that had brought him here. Originally he had aimed to collect his dough, which was not far away, then get clear of Onnaville. That had been his intention — until he started to think about Dave Arran. When he brushed past this newspaper man on the way to the elevator he'd done no more than congratulate himself on his luck. If Dave had been just a minute earlier, he'd thought, the setup would have been bad.

As soon as he was on the sidewalk he realised something else. Dave knew what he looked like. Dave would be able to identify him as the killer! Maybe it's a million to one against their seeing each other again, but could he take even that chance? He had gone through all this just so as there'd be no chance at all.

While Dave Arran lived, that chance existed. It'd always be on his mind. Wherever he went in the States he'd always have at the back of his mind that there was one man breathing who could send him to the hot seat. Just one man. A reporter, and reporters travelled around a lot. That meant that maybe the chances were less than a million to one. Reporters were natural snoopers, and could tell the world the result in a matter of minutes only. It was peace of mind that Pyro was wanting right now and for all the future. The peace that comes with safety. There was no safety while Dave Arran lived.

Even when he'd been standing there on the sidewalk he'd thought of going back to the apartment. Of putting a slug in Dave and then beating it out again, but there was too much risk in that. Pyro had known that Dave would get busy with the phone immediately. Subconsciously, Pyro squeezed his left arm against the place where his gun was concealed. 'I still gotta get that guy,' he whispered to himself. 'I've gotta do that before I quit his burgh.'

7

Rhona quit the apartment that night. It was natural. She took a room in the *Empress Hotel* in the centre of the city. Dave helped her to move in. It was getting late when he left the hotel. He had parked his coupé near the main entrance. As he was unlocking the door he was vaguely aware of three guys moving up on either side. One, who was much taller than the two others, was grinning as he said, 'Would you be Dave Arran?'

Dave said that he would.

'That's fine. You can call me Lex. We wanta talk to you, Mister Arran.'

Dave decided this was not a mutual desire. Under the streetlights he recognised all three of them. 'I know your name,' he said. 'But it ain't my ambition to use it. You skobs were mixed with Pyro until that guy went into the pen.'

Lex nodded. 'Sure thing. It's kinda easy to see you're a reporter. You know all the facts. Maybe you know Pyro broke out of the big house a couple of weeks back.'

'Yeah, some folks have a kinda feeling that you boys might know something about that.'

'Maybe, but that don't worry us none. There ain't any proof. We're gonna take a ride with you, Mister Arran.'

Dave was standing against the open door. The three formed a compact group round him. They started to hustle him into his car, but Dave was not easily hustled. He had plenty of poundage, and he had a few ideas on how to use it. Lex was the first to be aware of that fact. The information dawned on him when he felt something like a high voltage shock start in the middle of his belly and spread out over his entire body. It was a short left arm jab. As he staggered back a step Dave said: 'I hope you hoods ain't thinkin' of showing up tough.'

Lex said something that no nice, clean thinking American ought to say, but it was Rick who brought the argument to an end. 'You'd better do like Lex says. We ain't here because we appreciate the night air,' he said, and his words were not so persuasive as the gun in his hand.

There was plenty of caution about the way he was doing it. The rod was squat, of small calibre. Right now, it was almost entirely concealed by the folds of Rick's jacket. Almost — there was enough of it visible for Dave to see the muzzle aimed at him.

There are some guys who argue it out when they are threatened by a hood's gun. They are heroic. They are an example to all other citizens, and the citizenry most always show their gratitude by giving them a grade-one funeral. Dave didn't fall into that colourful category. He glanced along the sidewalk. A few folks were coming out of the hotel. They looked like they were in a hurry to get home and did not so much as look at the group. A cop was standing on a traffic isle a few yards further along. That was no consolation. Even a small calibre bullet can travel a lot faster than a cop.

Dave shrugged. He climbed into his roadster. As he settled behind the wheel Lex and Dal relaxed beside him. Rick got in at the back, his gun still out. Rick was not relaxing.

Dave was now finding time to feel curious. 'What is this?'

Lex answered: 'We'll talk about that later, bud. First we want you to drive a few miles outa town. You can stop at a quiet stretch of highway. What we've gotta say to you is kinda confidential. We don't want to be overheard.'

Dave took the north exit from Onnaville. He decided that this was a helluva day. Maybe he'd never complain again about life being too quiet.

After ten minutes' fast driving Lex said, 'This'll do.' Dave braked the roadster at the side of a wooded patch. He switched off the engine and waited. 'I guess you're kinda worried,' Lex continued. 'Well, we don't aim to drag out your agony. We can set your mind at rest. You ain't gonna be hurt — not if you're wise and move along our way.' Dave didn't answer. The ball was in their court and he decided to let them go on playing it.

Lex warmed to his task. 'I'm gonna unload a lotta facts on you, Dave. I figure they're gonna just get you. Here's fact number one. It was Pyro who killed the doc!'

Dave, who had been lighting a cigarette, dropped both it and the match on the floor. The hoods were grinning like they got some pleasure out of his astonishment. It didn't end there, however, Lex gave it all from the time they sprang Pyro out of the pen, to Juruski's operation on him and the escape.

It takes a lot to rock a newspaper man, but by the time Lex had finished Dave felt like he was swaying on springs. He knew Lex wasn't kidding. The story fitted in too well. It was quite a time before he said, 'Why've you told me this? If you ain't gonna harm me, it means I can go right to the cops.'

'You ain't goin' to any cops,' Lex told him. 'Not if you value the safety of that dame of yours. It'd be too bad if she had an accident just because you opened your kisser.'

Dave felt his guts turn cold. There was a lot of meaning in that threat. Those hoods weren't kidding. He knew the type.

They'd kill anyone — even a woman — with no more worry than the average guy feels when he swats a fly.

'Okay, so I've gotta keep quiet,' Dave said. 'But just why've you punks brought me out here and told me this?'

Lex laughed. 'You're slowin' down, newshawk! Don't you get the idea that we wanta find Pyro? We still want that dough, and we've a hunch Pyro will wanta see you. Maybe he'll have a plan for puttin' a slug in you, as you're the one guy in the world who knows what he looks like. We figure Pyro ain't been to all this trouble so that one guy like you can send him to the hot seat.'

Dave remembered O'Teefe's words, but that cop had only guessed the half of it! 'So you aim to tag on to me until Pyro comes along? No, sir! That ain't gonna work out. A lotta folks'll ask a lot of questions if I have an escort of three hoods every place I go.'

'We ain't that dumb' Lex said. 'We can be modest. We won't be seen — understand? We'll be around, that's all. We'll be close to you from now on for every minute of every day — until Pyro happens along. When that time comes you'd better bawl out his name loud, it's your one chance of stayin' alive! We gotta move before Pyro does. Get it? You sure had better! Say, you're no dumb-cluck. You get it okay,' Lex told him. 'You can take us back into town. You and that dame of yours have an even chance of comin' out okay, if you play this our way. If you don't, then we'll fix the dame, and I guess Pyro'll fix you. Think about that before you go to sleep tonight, bud.'

* * *

Pyro told himself, 'There ain't any reason for me to skulk around like some guy on the run. I'm okay. I've got a new pan. While I'm waitin' to fix Mister Dave Arran I might as well live in comfort.' He spent quite a while thinking about a new name for himself. He decided to pick something smart-sounding, but not too out of the ordinary. That wasn't so easy. When it came to the point he couldn't think of any names like that. In the end he had to flick through the telephone lists to find what he wanted, but he hit it at last — Farbridge. That was it. Colin K. Farbridge. A nice respectable sorta handle. That was who he'd be from now on. Mister Farbridge, Pyro was dead. There was no Pyro.

Colin K. Farbridge bought himself some baggage, and took a taxi to the *Empress Hotel*. It was there that he found that a new name takes some getting used to. The clerk pushed the register his way and he started to sign. He got the first two letters written when he realised his mistake. He deleted them heavily and started again. While the clerk was unhooking his room keys he leaned against the reception desk and looked idly across the hotel lobby. It was quite a place, the *Empress*. A good toned joint. The sorta place where he'd always stay from now on.

The bell hop said: 'I'll show you to your room, Mister Farbridge.' Was the guy deaf or something? The bell hop had another try, louder. 'I'm ready, Mister Farbridge.'

This time, Pyro realised that the kid was talking to him. It came like a shock. As he got into the elevator he started to get the idea that it was going to be hard work, this change of identity.

They got out of the elevator at the sixteenth floor and the bellhop, who was carrying the baggage, led the way down the thick-carpeted corridor. They stopped at room number 932. As the bellhop was unlocking the door a guy came out of the adjoining room. Out of number 933.

It was Dave Arran. He stood there on the threshold talking in undertones to Rhona, like he was reluctant to leave, and before he at last moved away, Rhona squeezed his hand like she was reluctant for him to go. Pyro, who organised a short delay in entering his own room, saw all this. He found that one of his shoelaces needed tying and he stayed in the corridor to attend to it, his head well out of Dave's line of vision.

Pyro, on entering his own room, gave the bellhop five bucks. He was feeling that way. Big and generous. The cards sure were dealing for him. Right now, his hand was all aces. This setup could not have been bettered if he'd planned it himself. Among his purchases that day had been a ready-made brown wig. It had set him back all of two hundred, but it was well worth it. That wig, now rested on his bald dome, wouldn't exactly kid anybody. Nobody would think he was a walking advertisement for a hair tonic, but it completed the work of Juruski. His vast bald scalp had been a striking feature. It meant that seen from the back, he still looked the same.

He crossed to the window and opened it. A ledge ran from just below his room level to room 933 and it continued along the whole length of the hotel building. It was no more than eighteen inches wide, maybe a bit less, and the back street was sixteen floors below. That was a helluva drop. Pyro gazed down towards the bottom of the black chasm. He remembered that he'd once seen a suicide jumper throw himself from around this height. He hadn't looked like a man at all when they'd picked him up.

Pyro had no intention of falling when

the time came for him to cross that ledge. His nerves were good. He wasn't scared. Just the same, it was a long time before he was able to get some sleep.

★ ★ ★

Dave braked his roadster outside the *Onnaville Star* office. He said to Lex, 'I'm going in here. I've got work to finish before I hit the hay.'

'That's okay, bud,' Lex told him. 'Just see you come out by the main door so we can keep tabs on you. If you're thinking of any smart moves it'll be too bad for that dame of yours, and you'd better get used to me reminding you!'

He got out of the car. Rick and Dal followed. The three disappeared among the shadows. Dave figured they were going to have a busy time watching him twenty-four hours a day. He eased into the office and crossed to his desk in the newsroom. It was now past one o'clock, and the night staff was at work on the morning editions. The editor looked at him hopefully. 'Got any more dope on the killing?' he asked.

'I haven't,' Dave said. 'I've come in here because I can't tear myself away from the place.'

He picked up the telephone and got through to the *Empress Hotel*. He asked for Rhona's room. She answered almost immediately. It seemed like she had too much on her mind to sleep. Dave pitched his voice low and spoke with his lips pressed close to the mouthpiece. 'Listen honey. I don't want you to ask any questions. Just do exactly like I tell you. It's mighty urgent and I'll explain later. Understand?' Rhona hesitated like she was puzzled, then said she understood. 'You've gotta pack your grip right now — yeah, right now. You've gotta leave the hotel. There's a train in an hour that stops at Stone Dip — that's sixty miles out. Get that train and book in at the hotel there. Don't let anyone know where you are.'

At her end of the line Rhona detected the urgency in Dave's tones. 'But you can't expect me to get up in the middle of the night without telling me why! What's the matter, Dave?'

'Unless you do just like I say there'll be plenty the matter. Listen, I ain't in any mood for a debate. You heard what I told you — do it, and do it right now.' There was a harsh, brittle edge to those words. She'd never heard him talk like this before. Rhona realised he was deadly serious.

She said very quietly, 'Okay, Dave, I'll leave now and get that train for Stone Dip.'

'Fine — I'll contact you there some time in the afternoon. But remember — you've gotta lie low. Don't start springing any parties for your city friends.'

Rhona said she wouldn't and pushed away the phone. Some of Dave's urgency had transmitted itself to her. She got out of bed and started to dress. Without knowing why, she felt scared. She did not have to know why to feel that way. Obviously Dave wouldn't have given this order unless there was some kind of danger.

She'd only brought one case of clothes with her. That was quickly packed. The

81

reception clerk raised his eyebrows when Rhona told him she was checking out. 'Aren't you satisfied with the service?' he asked.

'The service is fine. I've just had to change my plans, that's all.'

While making out the bill he watched her with fast, darting glances. He knew this was the girl whose apartment had been used for the killing. Now she was beating it at a time when most folks are asleep. He started to wonder whether she was as innocent as she looked.

Rhona paid the bill and walked across the dimly-lighted lobby. A janitor was dozing on a chair near the glass doors. She shook his shoulders and said: 'Can you get me a taxi? I want to go the station.'

At first he didn't look so pleased. He saw things differently when Rhona pushed a couple of bucks into his palm, and he said he'd call for a taxi from the all-night rank round the corner.

Rhona followed him through the doors and waited at the top of the marble steps. There was a square of gardens on the opposite side of the road. A few hoboes were sprawled on the long seats. She didn't pay much attention when one of these guys got up, stretched, then ambled towards the hotel. As he came under the lights she saw him clearly. It was then she noticed that this guy wasn't exactly dressed like a hobo. His clothes were good in a flash kind of way. All colour and padding. Rhona started to take a definite interest in him when she saw that he was approaching her. He was grinning as he mounted the steps. He stopped in front of her. 'I guess you're Rhona Hayle. That wasn't such a bad picture of you in the newspaper. I recognised you right away.'

Rhona watched his lean, strained face. A face that came close to being good-looking. He spoke with the accent of a college boy.

'What's it to you?' she asked. He wasn't discouraged.

'Would you be thinking of goin' any place?'

She didn't answer. She looked round for a sight of the taxi. The street was deserted. A pool of alternating dark and light. That janitor was taking a heck of a time.

Rick said, 'We had a hunch something like this might happen. Your dreamboy is full of bright ideas, but it isn't safe for you to start runnin' around this time of night. It doesn't look respectable. Maybe you'd better let me act as escort.'

Rhona decided she'd taken enough. 'If you don't get right out of my sight I'm going to call for help.'

He nodded. 'Sure, I know how you feel. But that sort of singing won't get you any place. You'd best do just like I tell you — if you wanta go on being young and healthy.'

Rick had a hand in his jacket pocket. He pressed something through it, and into Rhona's waist. She knew what it was. The knowledge didn't improve her confidence.

This was the first time she'd felt the pressure of a gun. There had been times when she'd wondered what this sensation was like — the sensation of knowing that a slight movement of someone's first finger would mean the end of your life.

Now her curiosity on this subject, at least, was satisfied. Right now, she knew that you don't think of resistance. You do exactly what you're told. A gun, she decided, was a great persuader.

'I guess you've sent the janitor for a taxi,' Rick said. 'That's fine. When it comes, we'll go for a ride together. But don't do any squawking. If you do, there'll be a fast pay off.'

He nudged her again with the concealed gun. The taxi cruised up, the hotel janitor riding on the running board. He looked surprised at the sudden appearance of Rhona's escort.

He said to the driver, 'The lady wants to go to the station.'

Rick didn't contradict him. He got in with Rhona, sitting close to her so she could still feel the gun. It was when they had drawn away from the hotel that Rick leaned forward and said to the driver, 'We've changed our plans. Drop us off at the corner of Buke Street.'

Rhona had heard of Buke Street — but only heard. It was in the part of Onnaville where the cops prefer to patrol in pairs and where the residents preferred them not to patrol at all. She said, 'What is all this? What are you taking me to Buke Street for? Maybe you don't know it, but this is abduction, and I guess it can earn you a long jail sentence.'

'Let me do all the worrying about that. You just go on being a nice quiet dame and you'll be okay. Maybe you'll be told the pitch in good time.'

The taxi braked at the corner of Buke Street. Rick paid it off. He waited until it had turned round, and made back towards the city centre before prodding Rhona with the rod. They turned out of the street and into another dingy thoroughfare. On either side there were dingy shops with untidy, and even dirty windows. The lighting was dim. It was the sort of district that stinks of garbage cans, and cheap liquor.

They were halfway along it when Rhona saw something for which she'd been hoping. A couple of cops. They had turned the corner right ahead, and were walking towards them on the same sidewalk. She felt that gun again. Pressed extra hard into her ribs. Rick whispered out of the side of his mouth, 'If you yap, I'll give it to you. I ain't kiddin' — I'll let you have it — '

Rhona was thinking fast. She put her thoughts into rushing words. 'You don't — you wouldn't dare. If you shoot me the cops'll have you before you've covered a couple of steps. I'm going to — '

They were in a pool of darkness between two streetlights. Rick used that temporary concealment. He used it to bring his left mitt up and across Rhona's chin. It wasn't a particularly hard punch. It couldn't be hard because of the angle from which it was delivered, but it was enough to slap the girl cold. She started to fold forward. Rick caught her before she hit the sidewalk. He held her upright while groping in his hip pocket. There was a whisky flask in there. Uncorking it with his teeth, he threw some of the contents on to Rhona's face. The liquor dribbled down to her costume.

He was dropping the flask back into his pocket when one of the cops directed a torch beam on them. 'What's the matter with the girl?'

Rick gave an embarrassed kind of grin. 'She's passed clean out. I guess she's had too much. I'm takin' her home.'

He put it over well. As though he was ashamed of the setup. The torch beam rested on Rhona's soaked face, her tight shut eyes.

'It looks like she's been swimmin' in the stuff. She seems a nice kinda kid, too. You must be a no good boy to get her in that condition.'

The other cop came in. He had aimed his light on Rick. 'Say, you sure are right about him bein' no good. This bum used to run around with Pyro.'

Rick was supporting Rhona with his left hand. His other mitt closed again round his gun. Both torch beams were on him now.

'Geeze! So it is. This is Ricky boy. We had a hunch you might be hookin' up with Pyro now he's broke from the pen.'

'I don't string along with guys who're as hot as him,' Rick said softly. 'I figure Pyro won't be in circulation for long.'

'You're darned right he won't,' the first cop said. 'Still, I guess this puts you in the clear. You wouldn't be on the run with Pyro and escortin' a boozed girl around at the same time — you'd better get her off the streets and do it quick.'

Rick said he'd do just that. The officers moved away. He picked up Rhona and slung her slim body across his shoulders.

Carrying her in that way he walked to near the end of the street, where he stopped at one of the shops, and producing a key, let himself into the musty blackness. There was a narrow passage with a staircase leading off. Still carrying Rhona, Rick mounted those stairs. He entered a room on the first floor, switched on the light, then dumped her on a settee.

Rhona's eyes flickered open. She started to cough as the liquor fumes caught her throat. There was a vacant expression about her, like she was trying to figure out what had happened. Rick stood opposite her. 'It wasn't so smart of you to think of yellin' for those cops,' he said. 'I had to slug you on the jaw, but it might've been a whole lot worse. Those cops weren't so bright. Neither of them'll make lieutenants. That was kind of lucky. If they'd got too curious, it'd have meant a shooting war, and you'd have been the first casualty.'

Rhona blinked around her, hardly listening to him. That room was not a comforting sight. The floor was covered by a gritty carpet that was a blue colour in the places where the bare threads did not show. The settee on which she was sitting was aged, and stained. In the centre of it a spring was protruding through the material. A couple of deep chairs were in the same condition. The wallpaper was peeling, like it was so old it hadn't the strength to remain upright.

Rick was following her startled eyes. 'Maybe this place isn't so luxurious,' he said. 'I've seen better myself, but it's quiet, and that's a big advantage, don't you think.' His tones were bantering. He seemed to be enjoying this.

Distantly, there was the sound of the street door being opened. Of feet ascending the stairs. Lex came in. He was looking tired. A cigarette hung from one corner of his thin and pale lips. He stared for a long time at Rhona, then turned to Rick. 'So the dame tried to skip?'

'Sure. That guy of hers musta tipped her off while he was in his office, just like you said it might happen. She tried to get smart while a couple of cops were around. I had to slug her and hand out the liquor routine.'

Rhona's head was clearing. The last trace of fear had now left her. Anyway, the last trace of fear for herself, She was aware right now of only one desire. That was to know what was happening. To know why she'd been brought here. If she knew that she had a hunch she'd also know the reason why Dave had wanted her to clear out of town. She got up.

She took off the wet jacket of her costume. Then she faced Lex, and her lips started to frame a question, but Lex got in first.

'Relax,' he said. 'You want to be provided with all the answers. You can have some of them. You're here as a kinda guarantee that your dream-boy strings along with us.'

He talked for quite a time and he didn't miss out much of the background detail. Rhona had to sit again while he was telling her why the Doc had been killed. He finished with a two-edged assurance. 'You'll be okay so long as Dave Arran don't run to the cops,' he said. 'All he has to do is to carry on as normal. That's all. Pyro will come to him. I know Pyro, and he won't take a chance on a newspaper man being able to pin the Juruski killing on him. He had his pan changed so he could have complete security. While Dave Arran's alive he ain't got no such thing — we won't have so long to wait. I figure Pyro'll try to fix Dave tomorrow.' It was casual, the way he said that.

Rhona took a step towards him. She grasped the lapel of his coat. 'Pyro will kill him, but that doesn't matter to you, so long as you find Pyro — you can't do it — '

He tore free her hands, and pushed her away. He was grinning. 'You're breakin' my heart. Now listen, sister, you ain't puttin' on any floor show in this place. I guess Dave Arran's okay for the rest of tonight. He's locked himself in his apartment, and Dal's keepin' watch. So that means you can sleep sound. There's a room for you on the next floor. Mebbe it ain't so luxurious, but it'll have to serve. You won't be disturbed — so long as you don't get any stoopid ideas about breakin' out.' He jerked his thumb towards the door. Rick gave her a push in the middle of the back.

She picked up her costume jacket and remembered that her travelling case had been left in the taxi. For just a moment she thought that maybe the case would lead to help coming.

Then she realised that its discovery would not mean anything. The driver had dropped them quite a distance from this place, but there were those cops. If she were reported missing they might remember and they'd pick up Rick. That might be too late. Dave thought she was at Stone Dip and he'd said he wouldn't try to contact her until the afternoon. Until then, no-one would worry about where she was, except maybe her office, and they wouldn't do anything about it right away. They'd think she was ill.

Rhona was thrust into the top floor room. Rick left her there, locking the door. It was furnished on the same general lines as the place below, except that there was a bed against one of the walls. Not a very hygienic looking bed. The shutters, which were closed, were secured across the small window by means of a stout brass padlock.

8

Pyro finished dressing, except for his brown wig. He put that on carefully. Then he checked his gun. It was a high velocity Luger and so accurate it was almost impossible to miss with it at under twenty yards range. Ten shells were there in the magazine. They looked snug and reassuring. He put the gun back in its shoulder holster and rang for room service. He wanted his breakfast sent up. Just coffee and rolls. Right now, Pyro didn't feel like eating too much. Not until this job was done.

The way he figured it, Dave Arran was almost certain to visit Rhona that morning. She would still be in a bad way. He'd be anxious about her. That'd be fine. Now it was daylight, he checked again on the outside ledge. Being at the back of the building, the street below was narrow and unfrequented. Opposite was the side of a cinema, with no windows.

There was as good as no chance of being seen during the few seconds it would take to ease over to the next room.

A bell hop brought up his breakfast. He'd heard about yesterday's five buck tip and he acted cheerful. He said, 'Mornin', Mister Farbridge. If there's anything more you need, I'll get it right now.'

Pyro said he'd be okay, but the boy was determined to earn a cut. 'I like lookin' after gentlemen. You know where you are when you're servin' folks in pants. But dames — D'you know, there was a dame in the next room who checked outa here at three o'clock this morning. Yes, sir, and she — '

Pyro was pouring the coffee. He stopped doing that after slopping some of it. 'You mean outa room 933?' he cut in.

'Sure thing. I was gonna say she was a blonde and — '

'Why did she quit?'

The bellhop was a smart boy and noted Pyro's interest. It wasn't an ordinary sort of interest. It was kind of intense. He figured maybe the guy had been hoping to do himself some good.

'I dunno why she quit, sir. She didn't give no reason. I guess they don't have to, so long as they pay the bill.'

Pyro tossed a buck at him. Just one buck. He wasn't feeling so good. 'Clear out,' he growled, and the boy cleared, but fast. He didn't like the expression on Mister Farbridge's pan. Come to think of it, it was a kinda funny pan for a fat guy like that to have. Good looking, but thin when it had no right to be thin. He went back to the room service kitchen brooding about it.

*   *   *

At around this time Dal was beng relieved after his all-night watch on Dave's apartment. It hadn't been such a bad night. He'd spent it huddled in a deep chair in the lounge. Dave had seemed kind of unconcerned about his presence.

It was Lex who took over from him. Lex looked around the room and asked: 'Where's the newshawk?'

Dal nodded towards the bathroom door.

'He's makin' himself smart for the office, I guess.'

'You can get right back,' Lex said. 'You've got easy work for the rest of the day. You have to keep guard on the dame. She tried to break out of the hotel so we've taken her into kinda protective custody.'

Dal whistled. He said: 'I sure hope she ain't gonna make any trouble. I don't like trouble with dames.'

'She won't hurt you none. I've left Rick there. As soon as you arrive, he'll be comin' along here.'

Dal said slowly, 'You're kinda expecting Pyro to show up today, ain't you?'

'Yep. I know Pyro as well as any guy knows the sonofabitch, and I figure he'll try to put Dave Arran outa the way fast. He ain't the sort to flam around.'

'Are you gonna let him kill the guy?'

Lex nodded. 'I guess so. I guess that'll be the only way we can be sure it is Pyro when he shows up. We won't recognise him any other way.'

Dal's eyes had narrowed. There was a wary and mean look about him. Even more so than usual.

'Then you're gonna persuade Pyro to take you to the dough — while I'm guardin' a dame on the east side of the city. Maybe that don't look so good for me.'

Lex put a hand on Dal's puny shoulder. 'You're feelin' hot about nothin', Dal. We're in this together. Someone has to watch the broad, but when we've hooked onto Pyro we're comin' right over to pick you up. Then we'll all go together for the dough. That's the way it's planned, and that's the way it's gonna be.'

Dal had a lot of faith in Lex, who right now was looking so sincere he might have been an anti-drink campaigner. He had even sounded like he was a bit hurt at Dal's doubts.

'Okay — but I'll sure be glad when you've gotten hold of Pyro,' Dal said, and he eased out of the apartment.

Dave came out of the bathroom. He was wearing a purple silk dressing gown and looking sure of himself. Lex looked sure of himself, too, but Lex had more reason. Dave went into his bedroom to dress, leaving the door open, so they could talk. He said, 'I'm glad you're here, Lex. I want you to be with me while I do a big piece of business.'

Lex was sitting on the arm of a chair. He asked, 'Yeah? What's that?'

'I'm goin' to police headquarters. I guess it'll save a lot of trouble if you come too.'

Lex liked to play a good situation the slow way. Any kind of situation. If he had a winning five in a poker game he liked to delay showing it to the table. He got a kick out of the suspense. It was that way right now. He said, 'You ain't gonna go to the cops.'

Dave laughed. 'I sure am, and no bum hood like you is gonna stop me.'

'It looks like you don't care about that dame of yours any more.'

'I care a whole lot, but you boys ain't gonna harm her any.'

Lex got ready to play his ace. He could see the back of Dave's head through the open doorway as he said, 'Maybe you feel that way because you tipped her to skip the hotel?'

Dave was pulling on his jacket. He spun round with it half over his shoulders. His face had gone a dingy white. Slowly, he moved towards Lex. He said through his teeth:

'Listen, you sonofabitch, what d'you know?' Right now he was standing less than a foot from Lex and his fists were bunched. Lex wasn't worrying any. Lex was giving himself a cigarette.

Dave's right arm streaked forward. He gripped the front of Lex's collar, jerked him to his feet. 'Start talkin' or I'll whale the lights outa you!'

Just for a second Lex looked scared. That was because he wasn't holding a gun. Lex was okay when he had his fingers around a rod. Particularly when the other guy didn't; artillery gave him back his confidence.

He said: 'Maybe you'd better not ride rough with me — or it might be too bad for Rhona — we've got the broad in a nice safe kinda place we took her when she tried to flip the hotel.'

Dave relaxed his grip on Lex's collar. The rest happened fast. He rocked slightly back on his heels, then came forward.

At the same time his right fist moved up and across the angle of Lex's jawbone. It was one helluva hook. It had more in common with an explosion than a punch.

Lex went back over the arm of the chair. He rolled twice after hitting the floor. Then he stayed still for a long time — it would have been for longer if Dave hadn't emptied a water carafe over his pan.

When Lex came to, his hand groped for his gun. That was instinctive, but he changed his mind before the weapon was out. There was the concentrated essence of hell in his eyes as he crawled to his feet. His emotions went back to the primeval ooze. Those emotions caused his voice to shake.

'That wasn't so smart, Mister Arran. If that kinda thing happens again that broad of yours won't stay healthy for so long — get me?'

Dave knew he wasn't kidding. He'd always known that Lex wasn't kidding. This hood was a killer, same as Pyro . . . same as all of the mob. They'd kill Rhona if it suited them.

Suddenly he realised again that he'd get nowhere by slugging it out. Except, maybe, to send Rhona to the city morgue. His only chance was to play along and hope — just hope that something, anything, would happen. He said, 'Okay, it won't happen again for just so long as Rhona's okay. But if she's hurt by you punks — then I'll kill you myself.'

Lex didn't answer. He figured that Pyro would settle the problem of David Arran. A few minutes later Rick arrived. He looked curiously at Lex's already swollen chin, but he didn't comment on it.

Lex asked Dave, 'Just what are you aimin' to do today?'

In spite of the setup, Dave grinned very faintly. 'I'm assigned to following up the Juruski killing. The city editor's expecting a nice story full of hard facts.'

'Your city editor's gonna be a disappointed guy. You're gonna have an easy day. You gonna pick up that telephone and tell him you ain't feelin' so good and you're spendin' the day right here in your apartment.'

'He won't believe that. He knows I was okay yesterday.'

'Folks get taken ill sudden, don't they? Tell him you've got belly trouble. That'll sound good. Folks often get belly trouble.'

'What's the idea of keeping me here all day?'

'So Pyro can find you easy. I figure he'll phone your office to try to snare you out some place. He'll be told you're at home and not so well. That'll suit him. He'll beef it right over here.'

Dave crossed to the phone. His throat felt like it was swollen and his tongue was dry as he spoke to the editor. Maybe he sounded as if he really was ill. He couldn't be blamed for that. No guy feels at his best — when he is planted as a target for a killer.

*   *   *

Pyro didn't spend long wondering why Rhona had quit in the middle of the night. He thought of a reason and it satisfied him. The dame had run out because her nerves were raw after the killing of the Doc. She was seeing things, being in a room all on her own. So she'd decided to find some other broad to spend the night with. That was pretty good reasoning, and the fact that it was entirely wrong was not Pyro's fault. When you haven't got the background you can't paint the picture right. Pyro decided he'd have to find a new way of contacting Dave Arran.

He phoned through to the *Onnaville Star*. When the news desk answered he said he wanted to speak to Mister Arran.

'Dave Arran's off sick,' he was told. 'He's layin' up at his apartment. Belly trouble. There sure is a lot of that kinda complaint around. If you ask me I wouldn't be surprised if that guy ain't got ulcers. Everyone getting ulcers. They're — '

Pyro put on sympathy. That newspaper guy had passed on some nice information, but this wasn't the time to listen to a homily on the state of the nation's digestive system.

'Gee! Poor guy — guess I'll go round

to his apartment and take him some Dr. Plumb's Belly Tablets. I got plenty. Where's the guy living now?'

The mug at the other end fell for it!

★ ★ ★

Rhona had made a discovery by pressing an ear to the floor of her room she could hear what was going on in the room below. She heard Dal arrive and talk with Rick. Then she heard Rick leave. By their conversation she knew that Dal was the only person in the building beside herself. She figured that Dal would be paying her a visit soon. No one had been in the room since she had been shut in six hours before. He was bound to come up to make a check, and maybe bring some coffee.

Her brain was working at high speed under the stimulus of desperation. She looked carefully around the musty room. Her eyes rested on the bed. Like the rest of the furniture, it belonged to another age. It was constructed of faced iron rails and on each of the four posts was a heavy knob around the size of a baseball.

Rhona tested one of those knobs. It was as she'd hoped. It screwed off its base. The threads were rusted stiff, but with a lot of effort she got it free. It was disappointingly lacking in weight, but she had no time to search for something more useful. There was a creak on the stairs. That would be Dal coming up.

Rhona flung herself face down on the bed, holding the brass knob under her chest. Then she started to sob. She put over a swell job. If a talent-spotter had been around she'd have got a try-out!

As Rhona had expected, he came up with a tray. She heard him put it down while he unlocked the door. When he was in the room he paused, looking doubtfully at Rhona. Then he said, 'That ain't gonna do you any good. You might as well cut it out.'

Rhona didn't cut it out. She went right on sobbing into the soiled pillow. Dal snorted. He was feeling on edge. Kinda worried about Lex and Rick. He still had it in mind that they might forget about him when they went after Pyro's dough.

It was an unsettling thought. Now it seemed like he was going to have to share the hideout with a slobbering dame. That was a bit much! He wasn't really equal to the situation.

'Gee! Pipe down!' he croaked. 'That row's enough to give a guy the heebies.' He poured coffee into the cup and carried it to her. He shook her shoulder roughly. 'Take some of this and dry your blubs.'

Rhona knew by the closeness of his voice that he was bending over her. She also knew that she'd have to play this hand smart. She had to get herself into the right position before she could get to work. Raising her head slightly, she eased off on the sobbing. Dal pushed forward the chipped cup. Rhona pulled free her right hand as if to take it.

Instead, she swung the brass knob hard at the side of Dal's skull. It made contact at a point just over the ear. For a moment Dal stayed upright, an expression of astonishment in his glazed eyes, like a guy who has just been told he's due for a tax refund. Then he slowly folded to the floor, spilling the coffee on Rhona's costume.

It didn't need any expert to see that Dal was going to rest for a while. He lay so still that at first Rhona was scared she might have killed him. She rolled him face up. He was breathing okay and that was a relief. She noticed a bulge below his left armpit, and didn't need to guess what caused that. It was a small gun as was fitting for a small guy. Rhona transferred it to the pocket of her costume jacket, then she moved out of the room fast. She was cautious as she descended the stairs. There was a chance that one of the mob might return.

That didn't happen. She took in a deep breath of relief as she opened the door and stepped into the street. It was one of those streets that are never busy at any time of the day. There were a few guys standing around the entrance to a poolroom. A garbage truck was parked at one end. That was the full extent of the activity.

Rhona remembered that the thorough-fare was to the right. She turned in that direction and started to run, hoping to find a cop. It's always the same. When you want a cop he isn't around. When you don't, he is. The main street was crowded; and there were streetcars clanging along the centre. She saw a telephone box, dialled the emergency number and told the operator to put her through to police headquarters

9

Pyro never moved until he figured it was at least middling safe to do so. That was why he spent a clear half-hour just casing round Dave's apartment block. It looked like a cinch. If a janitor was employed in the place he wasn't earning his dough. The lobby was deserted, and there was a nice quiet back exit that gave on to an alley. It seemed like he could get in and out without being seen, which was just the way he wanted it.

He circled that block four times before going in the main entrance. He didn't use the elevator. He'd checked that Dave's apartment was only three floors up and the stairs were a lot less conspicuous for a guy to travel by. When he reached the third floor, he paused. It was a small block and the corridor here was short. Dave's apartment was number twenty-one. It was facing him. He stood against the wood panel, listening. There was no sound from inside. It seemed a certainty that Dave Arran was alone. Anyway, that was a chance he had to take. He pressed the buzzer.

From now on, all hesitation was ended. He was going to work fast. His hand was on his gun butt as the door opened. Dave stood there. Pyro thought, 'That guy sure is sick. He looks like hell.' Then he pushed into the room.

This was where he'd let him have it. One slug before the guy had a chance to move, then out again. He'd be clear out of the building before anyone came to investigate the shot.

His gun came out, but he didn't use it. Something made him freeze still. It was a sound that came through the windows. A familiar sound, rising and falling. The sound of police car sirens. Because he was momentarily still, Pyro made a perfect target for Dave's short right hand swing. It contacted Pyro on the button of the jaw. He started to spin across the carpet and would have hit the far wall if it had not been for Lex, who caught him. He had emerged from the bedroom with

Rick. Both had their artillery out.

Dave figured that these boys could get along without his company from now on, but the boys didn't share that point of view. As he made a rush for the door, Rick stopped him. Rick bawled: 'Hold it, brother — or I'll drop you!'

He halted with one foot in the corridor and looked back into the apartment. There was nothing encouraging about the scene. Lex was supporting Pyro. Pyro was still in need of support, and Lex was saying: 'Let him have it — then get outa here. This place's hot. Someone must have tipped off the cops.'

Rick was watching Dave as he rasped back: 'Maybe he'll be more useful while he's still ticking.'

Lex got the drift. 'Okay, let's go.' He pushed his gun savagely into Pyro's back. 'We're all together again, bud. I guess that makes you feel good!'

Pyro reeled towards the door. He was recovering his wits but he still looked in bad shape. Urged by the guns in their backs, he and Dave turned down the short corridor. The stairs for the back exit were facing them. As they reached the top step, Dave tried to play for time. He knocked against Pyro, almost putting the still dazed hood on his back. Lex didn't go much on those tactics. 'If we're still here when the cops come outa the elevator there'll be some shootin' — and you'll be right in the way of the first slug,' he said.

They moved down the narrow steps and there was nothing slow about their progress. When they were on the first floor landing they heard, faintly, the bawling of the cops from above. A few seconds later they were on the ground level.

There they paused, grouped together in a bunch. Opposite them was the door that gave out on to the alley. It was open a few inches, but not enough for them to see much. This was a bad moment. One question was now in all their minds.

Had the cops surrounded the building? If they had, then they'd walk into a gun trap as soon as they eased out.

Lex decided on the line of action. He nodded to Dave.

There was sweat on his pan and his lips were stretched tight.

'You take a look out there — and don't try beatin' it. Remember, we're right behind you, bud, and from this range we can't miss.'

Dave had no option about it. He pulled the door wide open. He didn't feel so happy as he took a gander up and down the alley. It was clear. The cops hadn't gotten around to circling the block — if they ever intended to do so. He gave a reluctant nod. The mob followed him.

Lex and Rick put their artillery in their jacket pockets. Lex said: 'We're gonna walk kinda casual. We've got the saloon parked on some waste ground at the end of this alley and that's where we're headin'.'

Halfway along a guy emerged from the rear of a shop. He was carrying a sack of waste material which he dumped against the wall. He went back in without taking a second look at them. The end of the alley was bisected by a residential avenue. They reached there without hitting trouble. The waste plot was right opposite and so was the saloon. Lex was grinning as he opened the doors. He said to Pyro: 'So it hasn't worked out so bad after all, honey boy — Rick's gonna drive. You sit in the front with him and the newshawk. I'll take the back all to myself so I can watch after your interests, but first, I guess we'd like a line on where you've put that dough.'

Pyro had fully recovered by now. 'What dough?' he asked, and he made it sound almost convincing. 'I just dunno what you guys are doin' or what you're talking about.'

Lex clicked his tongue. 'You're all right,' he said. 'You have sure got nerve, Pyro. But you don't get away with that kinda pitch. Maybe the Doc did make a helluva good job on changin' your pan, but I still recognise you. Shall I tell you why? It's because of one thing no Doc can alter. That's your voice. I'd know you by your voice even if you hadn't tried to slug Mister Arran, like I figured you would.'

They got into the car. Pyro was breathing hard, like he'd been running a

116

long way fast. Rick was looking uneasy.

'We haven't time to sit around yapping,' Rick said. 'Someone's tipped the cops off. They'll be looking for us. I guess there's only one way that could have happened.'

Lex said slowly, 'Yeah — the dame. Dal musta balled it up. She musta got out somehow.'

Dave realised the probability at the same time. It made him feel a whole lot better. Rick had started the motor. He turned to Lex. 'We'll have to beat it outa town,' he said. 'But maybe you'll tell me where to?'

'Pyro'll tell you that,' Lex said. 'Pyro knows where he put the dough.'

Pyro was set on playing this the hard way. He still had plenty to sell and he was going to sell it dear. 'I ain't talkin',' he said, 'except on one condition.'

Lex told him to quote his price.

'I want my gun back and I wanta be in charge here again. Sure, maybe I did try to two-time you boys, but you were too smart, so we're right back where we started, except we have the flatfoots on our tails. I figure we'll all do a whole lot better if we sink the feudin'.'

Lex was doubtful. Very doubtful. 'I don't trust you any, Pyro.'

'Okay, so you don't trust me. But there's two of you, ain't there? I gotta play straight, haven't I? Play along with me, and I'll take you to the dough and — '

Rick cut in. He was getting desperate. His hands were making damp and greasy marks on the steering wheel. He was almost shouting. 'Geeze! Will you guys cut the double talk! If we don't move soon we'll run slap into a roadblock. The cops'll be pushing them up all round the city.'

Lex wasn't impressed. 'Pipe down. We've gotta know where to go first, and that's where Pyro has to help us.'

Pyro asked, 'How's about my gun, Lex?'

Lex only hesitated for a moment. He passed over the Luger.

Pyro grinned. 'Thanks, Lex. I thought maybe you'd see things my way. Take the west highway outa the city, Rick.'

There was authority in his tones. Like

he was again running the outfit. Lex noticed it all right. He didn't like it.

Rick asked, 'What about Dal?'

'We ain't interested in Dal,' Pyro said. 'From what you boys have been sayin', I figure Dal hasn't shaped so good. As for Mister Arran, we'll keep him with us. I guess he might act as a kinda protection. How d'you like bein' a hostage, Dave?'

'You're crazy,' Dave told him. 'The cops ain't gonna let up because I'm with you. I ain't that important.'

'Maybe not, but you never know — you might be useful.'

⋆　⋆　⋆

Dal felt like someone was holding his ankles and he was being dragged under a pool of water. His head was bursting and so were his lungs. He wanted to bawl for help, but he could not breathe. Then he opened his eyes. Like most pint-sized guys, Dal was tough. Inside of a minute he was pouring cold water over himself from a pitcher in the corner of the room. That helped a lot, and by that time he'd decided what to do. It was too late to think of doing anything about the dame. He'd have to phone the apartment. That way, he might be in time to warn the outfit. Dal didn't feel so joyful when he thought of what Lex and Rick would say. Particularly Lex.

Before hoofing out of the building, Dal went to a drawer in the living room. There was a spare gun and a carton of shells in that drawer. He helped himself to both, then hit the main street and headed for the phone booth. It smelled faintly of perfume. That wasn't surprising. It was the same booth that Rhona had quit not ten minutes before, but Dal didn't know that and maybe it wouldn't have helped him much if he had. After consulting the book he dialled the number of Dave Arran. The bell rang for a long time. Then a gruff-voiced guy answered. It was not the voice of any of the mob. It said, 'Yeah — who is it?'

Dal said, 'Is Mister Arran there? This is his paper speakin'.'

'No, he ain't here. This is officer Rogan

of the City Police. I guess you'd better speak to — '

Dal didn't wait for his advice. He guessed he could get along without it. He slammed the instrument on to its cradle, fumbled nervously for a cigarette as he left the booth, stood on the sidewalk for a while, smoking jerkily and thinking.

Obviously, the broad had tipped off the cops, and it seemed like Lex and Rick had got clear. Where would they go now? They wouldn't risk coming back to the mean street to pick him up. Not now that they were hot. Dal hadn't much faith in human nature — certainly not enough to believe in that possibility. He didn't want to lose all prospect of getting his cut of Pyro's dough, however, and there was just one chance of doing that. Dal decided to take that one chance.

He walked a little way down the street. Then he saw what he wanted. An elderly woman with a figure like an over-filled balloon was getting out of a Cadillac saloon. He watched her enter a hair styling emporium. He peeped in. She was being ushered into a cubicle. Dal figured that if he knew anything about dames she'd be in there for at least an hour. Maybe three or four. The older they got, the longer they took for their beauty treatments. Which was logical.

Then Dal looked more closely at the saloon. His luck was in. She'd taken out the ignition key, but had forgotten to lock the doors. The ignition was easily fixed, but the doors would not have been so easy in a main street.

Dal slid behind the wheel. He groped behind the instrument panel until he found the leads to the ignition. He wrenched them out and in a moment had joined the ends of the wires together. The red warning light went on. The motor was switched ready. He touched the starter button. The warm engine purred into life. Dal swung the car across the street so as to avoid passing in front of the emporium.

It was jittery work, this heading deliberately for the area of Arran's apartment. Like looking down the barrel of a loaded gun, but Dal figured he might pick up the boys before they were clear.

He knew where their car was parked, and if they'd only just left the building he might catch them. Might! Anyway, it was worth the chance.

Inside of five minutes he had reached the residential district. One more minute and he was cruising past the front of the apartment block. The sight there didn't help his morale any. A couple of patrol cars were outside and a crowd of rubbernecks had collected.

Dal took an acute left turn, then another in the same direction. That brought him into the alley at the back where the car almost filled the narrow space. Because of this, he had to drive slow. He reached the end and crossed the avenue.

There he saw the car.

He saw the outline of Lex sitting on the back seat, and there were three guys in front. That meant one of them must be Pyro. They'd got Pyro, and they were moving away. Moving towards the west highway. Dal decided to keep on their tail.

★ ★ ★

Pyro gave the route orders and Rick drove fast. As soon as they were outside the city boundaries they turned on to a secondary highway. Rick thought that way they were less likely to meet with cop patrols and roadblocks. They'd covered around thirty miles without trouble when Lex leaned forward and tapped Pyro on the shoulder: 'Just where are we goin'?' he asked. There was something almost pleading about that question. Lex knew he was no longer the key man. Pyro had taken over again.

'We're nearly there,' Pyro told him. 'We turn off just a mile along.'

'Yeah, but where is it. Have you got the dough buried some place?'

'Stop yappin' about that dough: You give me a pain. I've told you I'll take you to it and I've told you we'll make the split. If you ain't satisfied with that, I guess Rick and me won't mind losing your company.'

Lex's eyes narrowed. It was a smart move to talk about 'Rick and me'. It kind of divided the two off against him. Maybe that was what Pyro was aiming to do. Lex decided he was going to be extra careful

124

with Pyro. He wasn't the sort of guy to be two-timed twice. Not Lex.

'There's a big Cadillac saloon way behind. I've been watching it in the driving mirror for the last half hour.' They all twisted round to look throngh the rear window, including Dave.

Pyro said, 'It ain't a cop car. They don't use Cadillacs.'

'I know that,' Rick said. 'I ain't saying it's following us. Maybe it's keeping too far behind for that, but it's got me interested.'

'We'll know when we turn off,' Pyro told him. 'You'll find an ash track just past these cottonwood trees. Turn up there and stop.'

The track was so narrow that Rick nearly went past it. He had to brake suddenly and the tyres screamed as he pulled on the wheel. Thick woods were now on one side of them and bare, open scrubland on the other. This was not a picturesque part of the country, but it was lonely, and that was an advantage.

Rick stopped the saloon thirty yards along. He kept the motor running. Dave, who sat between him and Pyro, watched them pull guns.

There was, however, no need for the precautions. The Cadillac went past at high speed. There was only one guy in it, and for the brief second in which he was visible, it was impossible to see his face because his hand was up, like he was pushing back his hat.

'Nope — that guy wasn't following us,' Pyro said. 'He must have seen us turn off, but he wasn't interested. Anyway, there ain't no reason for any private motorist to want to beef after us.'

Rick got the car moving again. The track soon developed a tough gradient. On their left the scrubland got thinner and there were clusters of maize growing, as though at one time it had been cultivated. After half a mile they hit level ground again, and came to a small derelict sprucewood farmhouse.

It was easy, even from a distance, to see the place was derelict. The roof was sagging and most of the windows were broken. Weed was growing up the walls. The place had two floors and it might once have been a nice kind of rural residence, but not now. Now it seemed as though it was tired of existing and would not go on doing so for much longer. As they got out of the car, Lex looked at the building with a bleak eye.

'How did you hit on this dump?' he asked Pyro.

'I used it for a hideout years ago after a payroll raid. It was perfect. It's like everyone has forgotten about it. It musta been rotting for a helluva time.'

With Dave in front so they could see him, they eased towards the door, which was shut, but required only a kick to open it.

The inside was no more impressive than the frontage. In fact, it was worse. They stood in a small hall with a room on either side. The floorboards were suffering from advanced wood-rot, and a bunch of buckweed was even sprouting through one patch. Green moulds were growing on the walls. Several steps were missing from the staircase facing them.

Dave made his first comment since the trip started. He said, 'It looks like you bums have found the right kinda home.'

They didn't seem to hear him. They all were too busy absorbing the fetid atmosphere. 'So this is where you've stashed the dough,' Lex grunted. 'I hope it hasn't caught the dry rot.'

Pyro gave himself a cigarette. He ran smoke down the nostrils of his newly formed nose. 'You move too fast,' he said. 'The dough ain't here.'

Lex and Rick turned to him. Neither looked pleased. 'Geeze! Why the hell have you brought us here then?' asked the latter.

Pyro went on smoking. He looked like he was enjoying that cigarette.

Lex grabbed his shoulder. 'Answer, you paplouse! This ain't our idea of luxury living. I hope you ain't gonna — '

Pyro acted fast. He took the cigarette out of his mouth. He jabbed the hot end on Lex's hand. That hand came away from Pyro's shoulder with the speed of light. Lex rubbed the scorched skin and swore in harsh undertones, but now Pyro was doing the talking.

He did it fluently, and his words were

directed specifically at Lex. 'Next time you try getting tough with me I won't play party games. You think you're a big guy, Lex, but you ain't. Right now, you're like a bum playing poker for big stakes without a card in his hand. Without me, you're all washed up, and you know it. So you're worried about the dough, eh? Okay, I'll put your mind at rest. It's near this dump — very near. But we ain't collectin' it yet. See?'

Lex was deflated. That trace of a whine came back into his voice. 'I ain't tryin' to play tough. I just want my end of the dough, that's all. And if it's around, why don't we collect and move out?'

'I'll tell you why — because the currency's buried. It's buried deep. That means we've gotta dig. This area seems quiet enough, but there could be some hobo skulkin' around who'd see us in the daylight. That's why we have to wait till it's dark. Now d'you get me?'

Rick said: 'So it's buried, eh — whereabouts exactly?'

'You'll know soon enough.'

They went into one of the rooms,

keeping Dave in front of them.

Lex looked at the prisoner. 'I figure we can get rid of this bum now. He might've been some use if we'd run into the cops, but right now he ain't even decorative.'

'Sure,' Pyro said. 'But we'll wait for it to get dark for that job, too. We're gonna play for safety. But you could rope him up. I don't like seein' him with his hands free.'

Rick got a length of cord from the car. With it he secured Dave's hands and feet. When that job was finished Dave was lying on the damp floor like a trussed game bird.

Pyro looked down at him in an amused kind of way.

'Maybe you ain't so comfortable,' he said. 'But you don't have to worry. You won't be like that for long. Just as soon as the night comes we'll fix you for a long rest.'

Dave tried to smile. It wasn't such a good attempt. 'I shouldn't be so sure of that Pyro. Maybe I'll live to write your stinking life story in my paper.'

Pyro was about to answer, but Rick,

who was looking thoughtful, cut in, 'I wonder how Dal made out. I guess we've forgotten about Dal. Maybe he's being held by the cops right now.'

Pyro shrugged his fat shoulders, rubbed his eyes. 'We don't have to worry any about that sore shrimp. He wasn't so smart to let that dame get away. A guy who can't look after a dame ain't any use to us.'

★ ★ ★

There isn't a man living who hasn't made a mistake about some other guy's character. Maybe a character is the easiest thing to make a mistake about. Anyway, Pyro had fallen heavy in his assessment of Dal. Dal was no Einstein, but he was no dope, either.

From the time he started to trail the car he'd had a big factor in his favour. It was his ability as a driver. In that respect Dal was in the top grade. It isn't so easy to follow another car on a lonely road without being obvious about it, but Dal managed it well. He hung on at just the right distance and that was why the outfit had only had a passing suspicion, and that suspicion was allayed when Dal was smart enough to drive right past them while shielding his face.

He didn't drive so very far past. Not more than a few hundred yards. There he drove the Cadillac off the road and into the concealment of some bushes, from which he hoofed back towards the track. There were deep tyre marks that showed him that their car had moved on, but Dal did not travel up that track. He wasn't as dumb as that. He got himself among the cotton wood trees and travelled that way.

He did not emerge from the trees until he was past the house. Then he made a quick dart across the short open space until he was pressed against the rear wall. He had it all worked out. He was going to wait until the boys had actually produced the dough. Then he'd produce himself.

The next move was to find out just what they were doing. He heard them talking through the thin and rotting walls. The voices came from the front.

Dal eased in that direction. There were no windows at this side so there wasn't a lot of risk, but when he got to the front he stopped. The door was ajar and he could make out all their words.

His mouth hung slack as he listened to Pyro say that the stuff was buried, and would be dug out when it was dark. He heard Pyro say, 'We don't have to worry about that sore shrimp . . . ' Then he moved back the way he came until he was again concealed by the trees.

Sore shrimp . . . sore shrimp . . . So they didn't have to worry about him! The dirty double-crossing — Dal fingered his gun. They'd find out what sort of guy he was. Sore shrimp, huh? Geeze! Guys could get poisoned and from shrimps!

10

It was almost dark. Outside there were still a few streaks of light in the sky, but that was all. In the farmhouse where there was no illumination, it was pitch black. It had seemed like a long time for all of them, waiting in there, but for Dave, each minute had been a year. A man doesn't give up easy, even when a death sentence is rushing up to meet him.

Dave had just about done so. In the hours he'd tried everything — which wasn't a lot.

He'd tried loosening the cords around the wrists and ankles. Rick had tied them too well. The only result seemed to be to make them still tighter. As the shadows deepened in the room he had pushed himself towards a protruding nail in the wall with the idea of using it to rub through the bonds. That had been a faint hope, anyway, but he didn't even have the opportunity of trying it. Pyro had seen

him and handed out some discourage-
ment in the form of a kick in the ribs.

That kick had knocked him unconscious for a while. From then, he had
almost given up. He figured that when the
time came Pyro or one of the others in
the mob would let him have it the fast
way. There was no reason why they
should want him to linger. Maybe that
was poor consolation but it was the only
sort available, except for the fact that
Rhona was okay. It seemed a safe
assumption that she'd got away from Dal,
because there was no other reason for the
cops arriving at his apartment.

It came as something of a relief when
Pyro crossed to the broken window and
said, 'I guess we can start work now.'

That pleased the boys a lot. They
hadn't liked having to wait in that
decayed house. Lex had spent some of
the time skulking around the upstairs
floor, but Pyro and Rick had remained in
that front room.

'If we're gonna have to dig we'll need
spades,' Lex said.

He was looking almost happy now at

the imminent appearance of the currency.

'I know where there are spades,' Pyro told him. 'Let's go — and bring the newshawk with you.'

They pulled Dave to his feet, releasing the cords round his ankles but leaving his wrists lashed behind his back. As they followed Pyro out of the rear of the house Dave had to be helped. His legs were numb and near to useless.

Pyro went into an outhouse and came out with a couple of spades. Then he led the way across what had been a concrete yard, and on to the scrubland. He veered right until he was forty yards from the house and only a few feet from the fringe of the cottonwoods. There he paused, before going up to a tree that was bigger than most others. He laid one of the spades lengthwise against the base of the trunk, then measured three lengths from it. There he jabbed the blade into the earth.

'This is about the place. The stuff's dug deep. Maybe six feet down. It'll take you boys quite a time. You'd better make a long trench so's not to miss.'

The moon was rising. Its yellow light reflected on Lex's taut face. 'Six feet . . . that's a helluva way down. It musta been a big job of work for you when you buried it.'

'It wasn't,' Pyro said. 'I had help. Two other guys . . . They were nice kids, bnt you never knew them. They left my outfit before you and Rick came in.'

Rick said slowly, 'Aren't they due for a cut?'

Pyro grinned. 'Sure they are, but it wouldn't be much use to them. They ain't with us any more. They had an accident.'

Rick said, 'Maybe they had the accident soon after they'd buried the stuff?'

'Yep — as a matter of fact they did. I was kinda sorry, but I guess it was for the best. It might have been a big temptation to them to know where all this dough is buried.'

Rick took out a handkerchief and mopped his face. The night was cool but he wasn't feeling the same way. He said, 'Maybe it'd be better if you helped with the digging so either Lex or me could watch.'

Pyro chuckled. The chuckle that seemed to emerge from deep in his belly. 'So you boys are getting' scared, uh! I sure am sorry about that, but there ain't anything I can do about it. I ain't gonna dig. You'll have to do that. Maybe you've forgotten, but I'm a kinda invalid. Don't you remember — I've had an operation.'

Lex and Rick had taken up the spades. They were toying with the handles in a thoughtful way. Then Lex nodded towards Dave, who was standing near to Pyro. 'Maybe we oughta put him outa the way first.'

'Not yet,' Pyro said. 'He's gonna help dig his own grave. Maybe that'll ease the burden on you boys. When we've lifted the currency we can drop him into the same hole.'

Lex grinned. He liked that. The prospect seemed to wipe away his anxiety. 'Say, that's smart. Cut the hick loose.'

Pyro produced a pocket knife. He sliced through the wrist bonds. Dave started to rub his swollen hands. A pain like a series of high voltage shocks was going through him.

'He won't be a lot of use until his hands get right,' Pyro said. 'You two get started, and he can relieve one of you a bit later.'

Lex and Rick commenced to dig. They stayed facing Pyro though! Dave took a quick look towards the forest. The protection of those trees was very close. Pyro saw that look. He had inserted a finger through the trigger guard of his heavy Luger and was spinning the weapon round. 'You wouldn't make it,' Pyro said. 'But try it if you like, I'll guarantee to drop you before you've covered more'n a couple of steps.'

Dave didn't try it. He knew that what Pyro said was right. At the same time he wondered what kind of sense it was that made him decide to cling on to just a few more núnutes of life. Yet he knew that he would cling. Everyone clings. He'd even go through the humiliation of helping to dig his own grave in the hope that something might happen to prevent him getting a slug in the back of the head. It was a crazy hope, but it was all he had.

Lex and Rick were making good going. The ground was soft and they had already cleared a trench five feet long and about a foot deep, but Rick was getting tired. He tossed his spade so it fell at Dave's feet.

'You can take a turn,' he said.

Dave took up the implement. Standing beside Lex, he got busy. Rick was examining his hands. They were raw and already blisters were starting to form. He wasn't taking to this kind of work. Pyro moved a little back so that all three were conveniently in front of him. He was still spinning his gun. Inside him he was feeling good. Real good.

In another minute the boys would hit the dough. They'd be pleased about that. Rick would ease back to the trench so as to help lift it out. He'd let them do that. Then — Then he'd give it to them. His high velocity Luger had an automatic fire device, which meant that all ten rounds in the magazine could be sent off in just a shade over two seconds. Lex, Rick, and Dave Arran would be grouped close together.

A quick traverse with the rod would fix

them all like they were under machine-gun fire. He couldn't miss. Not from this range. After that, it was going to be easy. There would be no one alive who knew his appearance. He wasn't Pyro any more. Mister Farbridge would pack the currency and bearer bonds into the car and move off, but first, of course, he'd do things right. He'd give those boys a nice burial. The ditch they'd dug would be plenty deep enough —

There was a clanging sound. Lex raised his head and bawled, 'I've hit somethin' here.'

It was as Pyro had expected. Rick forgot about his sore hands and streaked back to the ditch like he was actuated by a spring. All three were huddled in a group as they lifted something from out of the clinging earth. It was a jerrican, the sort used in the army for holding four gallons of gas.

Lex called, 'So this is how you stored the stuff.'

'Sure,' Pyro bawled back. 'It's airtight in those things. But that ain't the only one. There's more.'

141

They found the others almost immediately and dumped them on the top of the trench. None of them seemed to notice that Pyro wasn't showing much interest in the dough. He had not taken a step towards them, but he had ceased twirling the Luger.

Right now, it was aimed direct at them. The boys didn't notice that, either. They had something else on their minds.

Pyro pushed off the gadget to fix the automatic position; took first pressure on the trigger. This was going to be simple, but he had to use plenty of care. In two seconds his gun would be empty. He didn't want to miss any of those boys.

Pyro brought his left hand up so as to give extra support to the barrel during the moments of fast recoil. Still they hadn't looked at him. He pulled back the trigger.

There was a lemon-hued flash from the gun's gas escape port. At the same moment the barrel jerked high into the air and ten slugs chased each other into the black velvet sky.

Pyro was aware of only one fact. It was that a sudden pain had entered his shoulder, as if a piece of white-hot coal and been inserted into it. That pain had made him miss. He was now holding an empty and useless Luger.

There was a clump of scrub bushes right behind him. He threw himself into them, and the impact sent a sear of agony through his arm. This he hardly noticed. He was already gazing through the leaves trying to figure out what had happened. Then he saw Dal. Only a shadowy silhouette, but Dal all right, maybe thirty yards away. He was standing on the edge of the forest, pressed against a tree trunk. He was holding a gun, a very small gun by the sound of its report, but it had done a lot of damage. Rick was sprawled face down on the ground, half of him hanging in the trench. Lex was on his back. Like Rick, he was motionless. And Dave? At first Pyro couldn't see Dave. Then he made out a figure rushing into the trees beyond where Dal was standing, and Dal didn't seem to be worrying about him. Dal was busy aiming his gun at the bushes where Pyro was crouching, and Pyro had seen enough. A lot more than enough. He figured this was the time for some action.

Pressing flat against the earth, he released the now empty magazine. He moved his right hand towards his jacket pocket for a spare clip of shells, but another spasm of pain went through his arm. He was aware of it this time. Aware of the fact that this limb was near to useless. Awkwardly, he got out the clip with the other hand.

He was pressing the rounds home when he heard a distant plopping sound. It came from Dal. Dal was aiming for the bush. Pyro twisted his new face into a grin. Dal's gun was too small to be effective at that range. He knew now by the sound that he was using a Derringer. The Derringer is a nice weapon in an emergency, but the emergency hasn't to be too far away. Not more than fifteen yards.

Pyro made a swift calculation. Dal, it seemed, had now used four shells. The first one had caused his own shoulder wound — if it had been fired from a larger sized gun it would have killed him.

Two others had been used on Rick and Lex.

They had been well within lethal range. The fourth had just been fired. The Derringer took six shells. Dal had two left.

There was another plopping sound and a small cylinder of lead, already losing most of its velocity, passed wide and high.

Pyro stayed very still. He was thinking fast. He knew he was invisible to Dal, although Dal must have seen him throw himself into the bushes, but he would have to wait before he fired back. That was because he wouldn't be able to aim so good, now he'd have to use his left hand. He would have to wait for Dal to come closer.

Dal obligingly did just that. With one shell left in his derringer, he slowly detached himself from the side of the tree, and started to move cagily forward towards the bushes, the tiny gun held ready. Moonlight struck across his face, which, Pyro observed, bore an expression of supreme confidence, even though Dal was acting cautious. He was kidded by the stillness of the bushes and the fact that there had been no return fire. This was the last time Dal would be kidded.

He passed the trench where Rick and Lex lay. When he was within twelve yards of the bushes he paused, gun levelled.

Pyro laid his Luger on the ground in front of him. With his good hand he picked up a small piece of rock, which he threw towards the edge of the foliage. There was a thud as the rock landed.

Dal took a half turn and there was a kind of desperate glitter in his eyes. There was plenty of cause for desperation.

He was caught in open ground. Pyro was still alive, and Pyro was under cover.

It was then that Dal was seized by panic. He did exactly the wrong thing. He fired his one remaining cartridge at the spot where the rock had fallen. As the sound of the thin explosion passed away there was a period of absolute quiet.

Quite a long period. During it, Dal gazed at the bushes like he was hypnotised. Then he heard music.

Slow, gentle, tuneful music. It was being whistled. It came from the middle of the foliage. Pyro stood up, lips pursed, still whistling. The moon glinted on the blue steel of his Luger. Dal gave out a whimpering groan. He squeezed the trigger of the Derringer and produced a futile click. It was then that Pyro stopped whistling.

'Nice to see you, Dal,' he said in an easy, pleasant kind of voice. 'I've been worried about you. I didn't want you to think we'd run out on you. I wouldn't wanta do that to a smart little guy like you. Not to a guy who can give it to Rick and Lex in the back — you're all right, Dal. But you're kinda quiet — ain't you gonna talk with Pyro?'

Dal gaped at the strange face. At Pyro's new face, but he didn't say anything. He couldn't. Pyro tried to encourage him. 'Relax, bud. You look kinda worried. You ain't got a thing to worry about. No, sir — all your troubles are over.' Pyro squeezed the trigger.

He was whistling again as he moved towards the trench.

11

Dave had to fight down a basic instinct — to keep on running once he'd reached the forest. To give praise that Dal's crazed hate had been directed only at the mob, so he'd been ignored; and to move as far and as fast from this hell spot as possible.

He couldn't have been blamed if he'd done just that, but that was just what he did not do. Instead, soon after he was among the trees, he forced himself to stop. Then slowly he returned to the fringe of the forest. At first he had to turn his head away. The spectacle on the stretch of scrubland was more than he could easily absorb. He watched Pyro walking away from the bushes. Watched him move towards the trench. The trench where Lex and Rick lay.

Dave looked back towards the farmhouse. He thought hard for a full minute. Then, keeping among the trees, he made in the direction of the decaying building.

When he was level with the front of it he had placed himself out of Pyro's sight. Even the moon didn't give enough light for one man to see another over that distance, and that was exactly the way Dave wanted it. He could make out the shadowy substance of the mob's car. It was parked a few yards beyond the house front. Dave crossed towards it, raised the bonnet flap, and groped at the motor. His hands found what he was seeking. They found the plastic cone of the distributor. He released the cover and removed the rotor arm. He was lowering the flap when he heard Pyro approaching. They were heavy steps, like he was carrying some big burden.

Dave glided towards the building and pressed against the wall. Although himself hidden by the shadow, he could see Pyro clearly enough, and he saw the reason for the heavy steps. Pyro was carrying jerricans. Dave watched him open the car-boot, and push the jerricans inside. He slammed the cover shut, then moved back in the direction of the trench. Dave waited. He had a hunch about the reason for the return visit. Pyro was aiming to play safe. Not to leave too much evidence about. After he'd been gone a couple of minutes, Dave moved again to the car — this time from the opposite side. He went to the back and turned the handle of the baggage boot. He cursed. It refused to open. He guessed it had one of the self-locking devices. He tried inserting the small blade of his pocket-knife into the lock, but that was useless. The tumblers inside were too well designed to be opened by that kind of trick. Time was passing fast. Pyro might be back at any moment. Dave started to sweat under the strain as his brain sought for some way of getting at those jerricans. Then he swore at himself. He did it softly but thoroughly. He had forgotten the obvious move, but that was often the way. Under stress most folks think of everything but the obvious.

He opened the car door and felt along the dash panel. The car key was there. The same key always opened the boot.

He took it out. The rest was easy. Easy up to a certain point. That certain point came when he had removed the jerricans and was about to shut the boot cover. He heard Pyro returning — moving fast — the sound of each step was louder than the last. Dave felt his mouth go suddenly dry, and there was a lightning stab of heat in the depths of his belly. Standing here right now, he'd be the easiest meat that had ever been served up to Pyro.

There was no time to take the jerricans into the forest. Pyro would see him before he was quarter way across the clearing, and if he took them any place else — He thought of a place — eased round the side of the car, and pushed the tins under the chassis. That car would not move unless it was pushed, and there was not much prospect of Pyro finding them.

There was no time to shut the baggage boot cover. That was a pity because if it had been otherwise Pyro might have waited a long while before he knew that he'd lost his dough.

As it was, Dave had barely the space in which to get back under the cover of the wall, where he did not linger. Moving on his toes, he crossed the front of the house. When he was well out of earshot he took a left turn and made down the gradient towards the road.

Several times he tripped and fell among the clusters of maize. It took him more than thirty minutes to reach the highway. There he moved more slowly in the direction of Onnaville. He hoped that someone would pass and give him a lift. He knew it was a slender hope. This was not a main highway. It was very secondary. He began to realise just how slender his hope was after he'd walked for a mile and seen nothing but the straight blackness ahead. He was feeling all in, like he'd been flogged by the whips of hell, when he saw a car. It was an old one, the kind of vehicle that's getting close to having an antiquarian value, but Dave was not particular about that. The important fact was that it was there, pulled up on the grass verge.

Dave stumbled up to it and looked through the glass panels. A man and a girl were sitting on the back seat. It seemed like they had moved there because it was more comfortable than the front. When a couple of folks want to have a serious talk they deserve some comfort. They must have been having a confidential kind of conversation because it was necessary for them to jerk apart as Dave rapped on the glass. Maybe it would have been more discreet if he'd given warning of his approach, but Dave was in no mood for discredon.

The guy pushed open the door. He was young, he was virile, and he looked like he was displeased. 'Say — you've a helluva nerve! Move outa here, will you, or I'll hand you the treatment!' He bunched his fists so as to emphasise the point.

Dave said: 'I'm sorry, I guess, but I'm in trouble — '

'You'll be in plenty more trouble if you don't scram!'

'I have to get to the cops,' Dave said. 'I have to get to them fast.'

The guy wasn't impressed. 'Say, who d'you think you're kidding? I ain't dumb. I know about you hobos pitchin' that kinda line so as to get a free ride.'

Dave couldn't blame him for making the mistake about being a hobo. Right now, he looked like just that. 'Look, I ain't a hobo. I'm a newspaper man and I tell you this is mighty urgent.'

'He don't talk like a hobo,' the woman said.

Her escort was, however, not convinced.

'Okay, if you're a newspaper man let me see your credentials.'

Dave hoped his press card had not been lost during the day. He didn't want to have to pull this guy out of his car,

Fortunately the card was still in his inside pocket.

The sight of it brought about a big change. 'Get right in,' the vintage car owner said. 'Sit at the back — no, not you as well, Susie. You come in front with me — there's a cop control station around ten miles along. I know just where it is.'

Dave sat back and closed his eyes.

12

Pyro spent quite a time looking at the open and empty baggage boot. It didn't take him so long to figure out what had happened. Mister Dave Arran was playing smart. That was obvious enough. The question was, what to do about it?

Arran had moved the dough. Pyro reckoned that a sucker like that would not have any intention of taking it for himself. Anyway, those three cans were too unwieldy to be carried far. Pyro had found that out when he had sweated with them under his one good arm. So it added up to one simple fact. Arran had moved the stuff so as to hide it, and that meant some place in the forest.

Pyro swore. Then he moved towards the trees. Somehow, in some way, he'd got to find that currency. He cursed himself for leaving it unattended while he worked with the spade. Who'd have thought that Arran would do anything but beat it for safety? Pyro decided that there was not going to be any more delay on his part the next time they met. The newshawk was gonna get it — but fast.

It wasn't pleasant in that forest. It was pitch dark, and a petrol lighter, held awkwardly in his injured right hand, did not afford either light or comfort. He wanted to keep his gun in the other. He moved in a straight line until he was deep among the trees. Then he moved back on a different but parallel route. His eyes ached badly from, he guessed, the strain of trying to see in that feeble and flickering light.

Having returned to the fringe he stood still, listening. There was no sound. No indication of where Arran might be. Suddenly Pyro became aware of a curious kind of fact. He didn't want to go on with this search. He didn't want to enter that forest again. It was sort of uncanny among all those trees. A guy felt helpless. Yeah, even when he was holding a Luger. You could be jumped on from behind and not be able to do a thing about it. Particularly when you had one bad arm.

Arran wouldn't know about that arm. Still —

At first Pyro was sore at his own reluctance. He couldn't understand why it was that he was so ready to let this currency be snatched from his fingers. All his plans had been based on getting away with the money — with all of it. He'd had the operation. He'd killed. He'd broken from the pen — all for that dough. For what? Just so some ham reporter could lift it outa his way when his back was turned? Now he couldn't be bothered to hunt for it. It was crazy. 'Maybe I am goin' nuts;' Pyro told himself, but he knew the reason. He knew, but dared not admit it even to himself. He was scared. Scared of the forest. Scared of the loneliness of this place. Scared of the fact that Arran was free, which meant the cops would be along. They might be along soon. Suppose he'd dumped the cans then hoofed straight for the road? He'd be running along that road right now, hoping for a lift. There wasn't much chance of getting one.

Suppose he were to drive down to the

road. Then maybe he'd see Dave Arran, and be able to persuade him to talk about where he'd put the jerricans. Pyro moved towards the car. Now that he could search without having to flounder among the trees he felt better. He slid behind the wheel and pressed the starter. The engine turned but it did not fire.

Pyro went on pressing. He was one of those guys who have no idea of what goes on inside an automobile. At first, he figured that if he persisted the motor would ultimately start.

After a while he began to see the error of that. There was a healthy kind of noise under the bonnet, but no useful activity.

He got out cursing, and raised the bonnet cover. Even his inexpert eye could see what had happened. Maybe even Dave's experienced ears would have twitched at the words Pyro used as he looked down on the loose distributor cover and the empty space where the rotor arm should be.

Then, very suddenly, Pyro felt the fever of panic. The same sort of panic that

Dave had felt an hour earlier, but Dave had fought it down. Pyro saw his own position. He saw the set-up as though he was a spectator and not a part of it. Here he was, without a car, without his dough, and with a guy who knew it all heading it for the cops.

Arran might be lucky. He might get a quick lift. If that happened the cops would be along at any time, and they wouldn't go through the formality of arresting him. They'd shoot on sight.

Pyro rubbed his eyes and sat on the car running board. His good hand was shaking as he flicked on his lighter and raised it to a cigarette. He'd inhaled the first draw and was about to snuff the flame when he saw something on the ground between his feet. It was a kind of impression on the damp soil. Like something had been laid there and pushed along it. Something about the size of a jerrican. Pyro dropped to the ground and looked under the chassis. Then started to laugh.

★ ★ ★

Captain O'Teefe was getting to work. He'd put out a tri-state emergency call. When Arran had spoken to him from the control station he had given almost all the information needed. He had given an exact description of the locality of the farmhouse and also described Pyro's new appearance. Already patrol cars were converging on the farm. Flickering lights on the big wall map opposite him showed that three cars were within five miles of the place. They'd be there in a few minutes. All traffic was being checked in the area. O'Teefe figured Pyro would get hold of a car somehow. He was not worried, in fact, he was rather pleased with himself. He'd be even more pleased when Dave Arran was brought into headquarters. In the last resort, Arran was the only guy who could positively identify Pyro. That meant that Arran had to be held in immediate readiness to rush any place where it was believed Pyro had been seen. O'Teefe glanced at his strap watch. It showed ten minutes to midnight.

★ ★ ★

Pyro looked at his watch. Ten minutes to midnight. 'If I'm gonna have a chance I've gotta move fast,' he muttered. There was nothing to delay him now. The jerricans had been emptied. The bearer bonds were scattered on the ground. They were a lot too bulky to carry about, but Pyro had got all the bills into his pockets without a lot of trouble. That was because most of them were in the high denominations. It was a pity about having to leave the bonds, but he still had a hundred grand in hard money. Pyro figured that was plenty.

He started to move past the farmhouse. He didn't know why, but he made a detour when he came towards the ditch. 'I'm getting' soft,' he told himself. 'There's nothin' to hurt me there. There's nothin' to see. I've filled that ditch in. It's all nice an' respectable.' Just the same, he was glad when he got away from it and was moving into the deep country.

His plan was simple enough. He was striking away from the road. When he was well into the scrubland he was going to turn west. He knew that ten miles along there was a small town name of Rombergh. He aimed to hit the place soon after dawn. If he got through his business there fast there wouldn't be a lot of risk. Not in that one horse burgh.

When a guy sits in a deep chair and thinks about it, a ten mile night walk across wild country seems to be no more than light exercising, but it seems to be a whole lot more than that when you're actually covering the ground. Particularly if you happen to have a slug buried in your right shoulder.

It was the slug that gave Pyro most of the trouble. The pain got worse. It got so he could think of nothing else.

Although the bleeding had stopped long since, he knew the wound was weakening him, and he couldn't afford to lose strength. He had covered maybe half the distance to Rombergh when he decided to take a close look at the wound. He hadn't had the time to do this until now. With difficulty, he peeled off his jacket. He was relieved at what he saw. The slug had entered the fleshy front part of the shoulder. And, because of its low velocity, it had not penetrated more than half an inch. Pyro was able to remove it with his fingers. It hurt, but not a lot. Once the lead was out, he felt a lot better. Except for his eyes. He'd have to have those eyes fixed. Juruski had blabbed about them.

As Pyro got closer to Rombergh the country became less wild. He was within a mile of the town when dawn broke.

He rested up for a while, sitting on the bank of a stream. The sight of the water reminded him that he was thirsty. He lay on his belly and drank deep. Then started moving again. He made contact with the highway into Rombergh and walked along it.

It was on the outskirts of the town that he saw what he wanted. An auto mart. It was composed of a square lot on which scores of cars were drawn up. A price was marked on each windshield. Pyro eased among the cars until he reached a small brick office. The guy looked like he wasn't fully awake as Pyro entered. His hair was ruffled and he had a kind of distant expression. He looked at Pyro with distaste. 'Yep — what can I do for you?' He sounded as though he wouldn't do much.

'I wanta buy a roadster,' Pyro said. 'It's gotta be a good model and I'll make it a cash deal.'

It's wonderful how the prospect of making a fast buck can clear a guy's head. The change in the garage owner's attitude was immediate. His fat pan suddenly became creased into a grin of sheer good humour. Even the creamy rolls of flesh under his chin seemed to pulse with benevolence. 'Gee — you couldn't have come to a better place, mister. You sure are smart to come here. It happens I have the very car for a guy like you. It's a De Soto an' it ain't been used much. Come right out and take a gander.'

He piloted Pyro out of the office. At the same time he looked with curiosity at the tear in the shoulder of his prospective customer's coat, and the blood stains.

Pyro noticed that look. 'I've had an accident,' he said. 'Piled my car further up the road. That's why I'm in the market for another. I've gotta have a car for my business — I'm a traveller.'

The garage man nodded. He seemed satisfied. 'Sure. Maybe you oughta have a doctor take care of that shoulder.'

'It's okay. I'll have it dressed some time.'

'Didn't you get hurt any place else — only there?'

Pyro said, 'That's all. I was kinda twisted round and thrown against the wheel. I've a few bruises, of course, but my shoulder's the only real hurt.'

They were standing beside a De Soto. The sale price of two thousand dollars was marked on the windshield. It looked okay for Pyro's purpose. 'I'll take it,' he said.

'You mean for two thousand bucks?''

'Sure I do.'

The garage owner looked almost disappointed. He liked to have a good wrangle over a business deal. This was something new to him. He'd never before sold a car for the price he'd marked up. If every deal was like this he'd make a lot of dough, but there wouldn't be much interest in life. Maybe there wasn't much point in it, but he decided to force over some sales talk. It'd be like admitting defeat if he did not. 'You've got yourself a high grade car here,' he said. 'It's equipped with most everything. It has — '

Pyro slapped a pile of bills into his hand. He didn't look like he was appreciating the conversation. 'Here's your dough,' he said. 'My name's Farbridge. I live at Marilyn Avenue, Brooklyn, New York. Make me out a pink slip and let me get on my way.'

The garage owner rubbed his already ruffled head. He couldn't figure this guy out, but he drew out a pad of official pink ownership slips, and started to fill it in with Pyro's fictitious name and address. While he was doing so, Pyro got behind the wheel. The man of commerce decided to make one more attempt to break down this resistance barrier. He wanted the buyer to listen to him — if only for a few seconds.

Still holding the slip he said: 'I was sayin', mister, this model has everything. A heater and a cooler, too. There's a new type radio with long reception.'

He pushed a hand into the car. The radio came on.

Which was unfortunate for the garage owner. Unfortunate because an announcer was putting over the news flashes, and it happened that right now he was handing it out hot.

' . . . this man is dangerous,' he was saying, and you could hear him savouring each word. 'He is believed still in the area of Onnaville and may try to get hold of a car. His description is — '

The garage owner's jaw was unhinged as he listened. That description — it sure fitted —

Pyro was starting the motor. He wasn't worrying about the radio. The garage owner said: 'Say, maybe you'd better hang around. Maybe I don't wanta do business with you — '

He broke off abruptly. He broke off because he saw Pyro's Luger. He saw that it was aimed at his chest. He even saw the hammer move back before it hit the cartridge.

Pyro pressed hard on the gas pedal. Through the driving mirror he saw for a moment the huddled figure of the man he had just shot. He'd left the garage behind when that same figure crawled towards the brick office and pulled down the telephone.

Pyro didn't shoot so good with his left hand.

★ ★ ★

He didn't drive so good, either. His right arm was still almost useless. He could only use it for brief seconds when he had to shift gear, and his eyes were aching, too. They'd never stopped aching in the last twelve hours, but somehow he had to keep moving. He'd got it all figured out. Right now, he'd be out of the area of roadblocks. That meant as long as he kept moving he'd be okay. So he'd keep moving. Until he was over the Mexico border. Then he'd be okay.

They wouldn't be looking for him in Mexico. Six hours would do it, and he knew a place where he could leave the car and get over the border quietly.

It was working out all right for Pyro.

He only wished one thing. He wished he didn't feel so sick.

★ ★ ★

O'Teefe banged down the telephone and looked at Dave.

'He's been contacted,' he said. 'He took a car outside Rombergh then shot the garage owner, but that guy's gonna be okay. Pyro's aim ain't so good these days. Maybe he's gettin' jittery.'

Dave asked: 'Which way's he heading?'

'I dunno, but we've got a description of the car and its licence number. It'll be picked up before long.'

The office door opened. A clerk came in with a typed message. O'Teefe read it and stood up. 'This is where we move,' he said. 'Pyro's car has been reported headin' south towards the border.'

★ ★ ★

Pyro knew it wasn't going to be so easy. He'd known that for the past hour. Ever since he'd heard the news flashes on the radio about how he had failed to kill that garage bum. He cursed himself, but that didn't do any good. That only burned up energy. Still, he figured he could make out. He was less than a dozen miles from the place where he was going to abandon the car and cross the border on foot.

The only big obstacle was driving over the mountain. He knew the mountain. It took him to the best place for making the crossing and dumping the car.

He could see the mountain road ahead of him when he also saw something else. In the mirror he saw a cop car. There was no doubt about it belonging to the law. It was cream coloured and there was a searchlight on the roof.

It was close. Less than three hundred yards separated them. Pyro wondered why he hadn't seen it before. He must be tired. He pressed the gas pedal flat to the floor. The De Soto had a powerful motor. It pulled up the side of the mountain without much loss of speed, but the cop car was gaining. Looking again through the mirror, Pyro recognised two of the guys in that car. One was O'Teefe. The other Dave Arran — and they weren't shooting. They were just following him. Like they thought shooting wasn't necessary, and they were right. A guy can't drive and turn back to use a gun at the same time.

Pyro's good arm was throbbing under the strain of holding the wheel, but that wouldn't be for much longer. He guessed he could fix this. He'd wait until he had. almost passed over the precipice ledge. At one part, there was a bend in that route. It was going to be easy. As soon as he was round that bend he'd stop his car and leave it blocking the track.

The cop car wouldn't have a chance. It'd slap right into the De Soto and be thrown over the side. Pyro achieved a grin at the prospect. That grin got deeper and he started to laugh, too, as he came out on to the narrow precipice track. On his left there was a vertical wall of rock. On his right the sheer drop of a thousand feet into a canyon.

He glanced in the driving mirror. The cop car was still quite a way behind. Far enough for him to get clear in time to watch the crash. He figured the crash would be spectacular.

His eyelids were feeling heavy. Like a slab of lead had been stuck on each of them. It was kind of hard to keep them open. They wouldn't keep open. They were shutting down. The muscles there would not answer his brain. They were throbbing, like they were exhausted, but he'd reached the bend. Though he could only see through narrow slits, he got the car round it, and braked to a stop.

He fumbled for the door handle, and somehow he got out. He was standing on the track, ready to beat it clear, but he could hardly see now. Those slits of light were getting more narrow every second. He used his good hand to try to force the eyelids up. Somehow they wouldn't move, but he had to move! Had to. Or he'd be sandwiched hetween the De Soto and the cop car.

He put out a hand. Maybe if he could feel the front of the De Soto he'd know which way to go, but he couldn't find it. His hand was just waving in the air. Pyro stumbled forward a few steps. Just a few. Then he stopped. He heard the sound of the approaching car. It was almost on him. He had moved in the wrong direction. Moved towards it. He gestured in a crazy way with his left arm. Then he screamed. His words were like those of a mad woman. 'I can't see — I'm blind — blind like the Doc told me — '

He turned so as to stumble back. He took three weaving, uncertain steps and each was accompanied by wild sobs. Three steps that made contact with the ground. With the fourth his foot met nothing. Just nothing. He was falling — falling in a black pit!

★   ★   ★

The driver of the cop car was no ham at handling a wheel, but even he would not have been able to avoid crashing into the De Soto — if Pyro had not come stumbling round the bend and forced him to brake. Dave and Captain O'Teefe stood on the edge of the track for quite a while. It was O'Teefe who broke the silence. He said: 'That louse had his eyes tight shut, and he was bawlin' somethin' about it bein' like the Doc told him. I guess he musta gone nuts.'

THE END

We do hope that you have enjoyed reading this large print book.

Did you know that all of our titles are available for purchase?

We publish a wide range of high quality large print books including:
Romances, Mysteries, Classics
General Fiction
Non Fiction and Westerns

Special interest titles available in large print are:
The Little Oxford Dictionary
Music Book, Song Book
Hymn Book, Service Book

Also available from us courtesy of Oxford University Press:
Young Readers' Dictionary
(large print edition)
Young Readers' Thesaurus
(large print edition)

For further information or a free brochure, please contact us at:
Ulverscroft Large Print Books Ltd.,
The Green, Bradgate Road, Anstey,
Leicester, LE7 7FU, England.
Tel: (00 44) **0116 236 4325**
Fax: (00 44) **0116 234 0205**

THE MISSING
HEIRESS MURDERS

John Glasby

Private eye Johnny Merak's latest client, top Mob man Enrico Manzelli, has received death-threats. A menacing man himself, he pressures Johnny to discover who was sending them — and why. Then Barbara Minton, a rich heiress, disappears, and her husband turns to Johnny. Despite Manzelli's ultimatum — that Johnny should focus on his case alone — he takes the job. But that's before he discovers the fate of the first detective Minton hired. And more bodies are stacking up . . .

A THING OF THE PAST

John Russell Fearn

Something was wrong, in and around London. Men were not shaving; women were becoming slipshod, dowdy and sullen-faced. People were bad-tempered, lacking self respect, and crime was on the increase. And, linked to these strange evidences of atavism, was a one-time excavation site. Now a mighty smoking crater, it looked as though a meteorite had descended . . . and from the vast fissure below the crater, there emerged the hideous survivors of a lost age of monster dinosaurs . . .

THE BLACK TERROR

John Russell Fearn

Troubled man Martin Clegg has always suffered from dreams which seem intensely real. In them, bizarrely, he's another person — not of this Earth! He's finally forced to confide in his fiancée, Elsie Barlow, and they consult Martin's scientifically inclined friend Tom Cavendish. He reveals, astonishingly, that Martin has a cosmic twin to whom he's mentally linked. Unsuspecting, they are about to become caught up in the strands of an incredible cosmic mystery that will, inexorably, be played out . . .